CHRISTMAS IN
QUINCY

USA TODAY BESTSELLING AUTHOR
DEVNEY PERRY

CHRISTMAS IN QUINCY

Copyright © 2020 by Devney Perry LLC

ISBN: 978-1-950692-33-0

Editing & Proofreading:

Elizabeth Nover, Razor Sharp Editing

www.razorsharpediting.com

Julie Deaton, Deaton Author Services

www.facebook.com/jdproofs

Judy Zweifel, Judy's Proofreading

www.judysproofreading.com

ALSO BY DEVNEY PERRY

Tin Gypsy Series

Gypsy King

Riven Knight

Stone Princess

Noble Prince

Runaway Series

Runaway Road

Wild Highway

Quarter Miles

Forsaken Trail

Dotted Lines

Standalones

Rifts and Refrains

CHAPTER ONE

CLEO

"Welcome to The Eloise Inn," the young woman behind the reception counter greeted. "Checking in?"

"Yes. Cleo Hillcrest." I plopped my Chanel handbag on the counter, slumping into the mahogany tower as I breathed a sigh of relief.

I made it. My suitcase rested against my calf, much like me, too weary to stand on its own.

"Let me just pull up your reservation." The woman typed quickly, the smile on her pretty face soft and sweet. The silver name tag on the lapel of her black blazer caught the warm light from the chandelier above.

"Thanks, um . . . Eloise? As in the—" My finger twirled in the air, indicating the stately hotel.

"Yep." She laughed. "My great, great grandmother,

Eloise Eden. The inn was named for her by my great, great grandfather. She was my namesake."

"Ah. Well, it's beautiful. The inn and your name."

"Thank you." Her smile widened. "I take pride in both. I'm the manager here."

"Impressive." It was possible that she just had great genes, or a miracle skin cream, but with her flawless, youthful skin, I'd peg her in her early twenties.

As Eloise returned to her task, a wood fire crackled in a large hearth on one side of the grand room. The hotel's lobby was decked out for Christmas, the mantel piled high with pine boughs and ornaments. Above the fireplace, a stone column towered to the rafters and in its center hung a wreath at least three feet in diameter.

Golden bulbs framed the windows. Inside the door, a fir tree three times the size of my car greeted customers with its woodsy scent and red bows. Tiny boxes, individually wrapped, were staged on a brass platter beside my handbag.

As far as Christmas escapes went, I'd chosen my destination well. Not that I'd ever escaped Christmas before.

But this year, Quincy, Montana, was going to be my hideaway.

"Okay, Ms. Hillcrest." Eloise looked up from her computer screen with another welcome smile. "I have you here for three nights. Checking out on the twenty-sixth. Is that correct?"

"Yes, it is." I nodded, fishing out my wallet for my driver's license and credit card.

"Are you visiting someone in Quincy for the holiday?" she asked, swiping my card through the reader.

"Oh, um . . . no." Exactly the opposite. I was in Quincy to avoid anything that resembled visiting. It probably seemed strange—it was strange—but since I didn't have the energy to explain the disaster that was my family at Christmas, I changed the subject. "When I called and made my reservation, I was told that room service would be available each day."

"Yes, of course. The menu and meal hours will be in your room's booklet. And our chef, who happens to be my brother, has something lovely planned for Christmas and Christmas Eve. We're happy to bring it to your room, but if you'd like to come down, the dining room will be open as well, starting at five and closing at nine."

"Perfect." I took the key card from her outstretched hand and collected my purse.

"Have you been to Quincy before?" Eloise asked.

"No, this is my first visit."

"Well, if you feel like exploring, we're in the heart of downtown. There are some lovely restaurants and shops on Main Street, most owned by local families."

Much like the hotel. The charm of The Eloise Inn was not something you'd find at a large hotel conglomerate. It had those personal, loving touches that made it perfect for my impromptu escape.

3

"Are there any bakeries in town?" While I was here, I might as well do some research.

"The coffee shop puts out a case of pastries and breakfast sandwiches each morning. If you like chocolate—"

"Who doesn't."

Eloise laughed. "The chocolate croissant is incredible."

"Sold."

"Head out the front doors and take a right. It's the cute green building across the street, three doors down. Eden Coffee."

"Eden?" I cocked my head. Wasn't that her last name?

"Full disclosure, my sister owns the coffee shop and is the pastry chef, so I'm biased. But she truly is talented. My great, great grandfather founded Quincy. My family has lived here ever since. You can't throw a rock without hitting an Eden."

"Good to know." I smiled. Five generations and the Edens were probably this town's royal family. "Thanks for the recommendation."

"I'm here if you need others." She took one of the gift boxes from the tray and handed it over. Then she leaned closer to the counter, stretching her arm as she pointed down the hallway. "Elevator is there. You're in room fourten. Take a left when you get off the elevator and your room is at the end of the hallway. Can I have anything sent up?"

"Champagne." My mouth watered at the thought of

slipping into some pajamas and sipping one or two glasses of bubbly before bed. "The most expensive bottle you have."

"I'll send it right up."

"Thank you." I gave Eloise a nod, then collected my things. A wave of exhaustion ran over my shoulders as I made my way toward the elevator. It was only six o'clock—five in California—but I'd been up since four in the morning and was ready to be done with this day.

The elevator's foyer was lined with potted evergreens, each lit by tiny white twinkle lights. Across from the silver doors, a wreath hung above a table adorned with faux gifts. The decorations were charming and traditional. Simple. There was no mistaking the season, but the tasteful ambience was a far cry from the overwhelming display at my father's house in Malibu.

My stepmother, Selene, picked a color theme each year and hired a company to splash it everywhere. When I'd gone over for dinner two weeks ago, the abundance of pink and purple—Selene's *unique pop*—had given me a splitting headache. That, and the apple cinnamon potpourri she bought in bulk this time of year.

All of it was staged for endless parties lasting days before Christmas and well into the new year.

I just . . . I couldn't do it. Not this year. I couldn't stomach the tacky—yet expensive—displays. The endless gifts. The hours of mingling with rich snobs and feigning smiles for pretentious guests. The only reason people spoke to me at those parties was because they thought I could get them an hour on my father's elusive and jam-packed schedule. Or that by kissing my ass, it would help them earn a promotion.

When Selene's magenta invitation for the holiday lineup had graced my mailbox, I'd thrown it in the trash and booked a plane ticket to Montana.

The elevator doors chimed as they opened and I hauled myself inside the car, inhaling a deep breath of pine and citrus. The mixture was soothing and special, the way Christmas was supposed to smell. There was no music as it whisked me to my floor, and when I stepped out, the same subtle scent carried down the hallway to my room. When I pushed open the door to room 410, I nearly cried.

It was . . . perfection. Exactly as I'd imagined. Precisely what I'd hoped for.

Delightful. Quiet. Airy, yet it held a cozy appeal.

The bedside lamp was on and a black shoebox looped with a red satin ribbon sat on the foot of the bed. The curtains were drawn and beyond the window the night was black except for a faint glow coming from the surrounding businesses and homes in the small town. Unlike the lobby and common areas, the room didn't have a hint of Christmas flair.

I propped my suitcase against the wall inside the door, dropped my purse on the bed and untied the ribbon on the box. A pair of plush white slippers greeted me from inside. I pulled them out and ran my fingers over the soft faux fur.

So this was why they'd asked for my shoe size when I'd called to make the reservation. "Score one for The Eloise Inn."

I popped open the top of the box Eloise had given me. Inside was a dainty chocolate truffle. "Score two."

I'd stayed at countless five-star hotels in my life, and so far, The Eloise was keeping up. Not to mention the price tag for this weekend escape was a fraction of what I would have spent elsewhere.

Despite what everyone assumed about me—Cleo Hillcrest, only daughter of tech mogul and billionaire Ray Hillcrest—I wasn't frivolous with my money. I was paying for this room on my own, with wages I'd earned, not inherited. I'd flown to Quincy on three commercial flights, though I had splurged for first class.

This trip was the only vacation I'd taken in years and a Christmas gift to myself.

My phone dinged in my coat pocket and I set the slippers aside to take the call. The bakery's number flashed on the screen. "Hey."

"Hey. Did you make it?" Brynne asked.

I sat on the edge of the bed, kicking off my heels. "Made it. How did everything go today?"

"Just fine," she said. "It was busy with all the people doing their Christmas-Eve Eve pickups. But we had a good day at the till. The display case is nearly empty."

"Oh boy." A pang of guilt hit hard. "Do you think I left enough in the walk-in to get it refilled? You might have to make a new batch of sugar—"

"Cleo." She stretched my name as she cut me off. "Don't worry. I can handle the shop. Come tomorrow morning, the display case will be full. You enjoy the next few days and let me handle it."

I sighed, sliding on a slipper. "I'm not doubting you. I'm just . . . I suck at vacations."

"Yes." She laughed. "I know."

Brynne had worked at my bakery for three years. She was an incredibly talented pastry chef as well as a wonderful friend. She knew how much Christmas stressed me out, and this vacation to Quincy had been her idea. She'd come here once, stayed in this very hotel and promised me I'd love a few days in the charming town.

"Okay. Call me if you need anything." All I had planned for the next three days was burrowing deep into this pillow-top mattress and watching as many Hallmark movies as I could.

"Unless the building floods or burns down, I'm not calling you," Brynne said. "Have fun. Sleep. Relax."

I slid on the other slipper and scooted deeper into the bed. "Thank you."

"You're welcome."

"Did you at least miss me a little bit today?" Searching for compliments wasn't a good color on me, but in my defense, I'd had a really long day.

"When I had a guy yell at me because he ordered a chocolate cream pie but wanted apple, yeah, I missed you. And when I burned my hand on the oven because I was in a hurry, I missed you a lot. You make the best ice packs. But today was a good day. And tomorrow will be a good day. I like that I can run this place alone. It's a challenge but I'm up for it, so thanks for trusting me with this opportunity."

Oh, she was good. Now I felt guilty for not leaving her in charge of the bakery sooner. "You're the best. Merry Christmas."

"Merry Christmas. See you later this week."

I tossed the phone aside and glanced around the room. Coming here, leaving California, was like stepping into another world. Outside, the snow was falling, blanketing everything in a fluffy layer. It would be easy to stay for days and days, relaxing inside this room and pretending the outside world didn't exist. But three days, that's all I had. I'd missed today at the bakery and wouldn't be there for Christmas Eve. We were closed on Christmas Day and my flight home was first thing the following morning. Three workdays was not a long break, but Brynne had been right.

I hadn't taken a vacation since I'd opened Crumbs five years ago. Mostly because I hadn't had anyone to run the shop before Brynne, and even with her, I liked being tied to my confections and creations.

Crumbs wasn't just my job, it was my passion.

I stripped off my coat, tossing it to the floor, and scooted into the pillows. The king-sized sleigh bed was a rich mahogany. The cream comforter was thick enough to swallow me whole—I planned on letting it. The pillows were fluffy and abundant. A television rested on a wide chest of drawers across from the bed.

This room was bliss. It was classy and there wasn't a bit that seemed hotel generic, even the furniture. When I'd called to make my reservation, the clerk—maybe it had been Eloise herself—had told me that I'd snagged the last room. Even though the inn was full, there wasn't a noise beyond the door, likely because of the thick carpet in the hallway.

The artwork on the wall over my shoulder was a black and white photograph of Quincy from 1950, according to the date in the corner. It looked similar to the town I'd arrived in, though it had been nearly dark when the plane's wheels had touched down. Still, there was something peaceful about knowing that the town hadn't changed all that much, decade after decade.

I pushed myself up and off the bed, moaning with pleasure as my feet sank into the thick soles of the slippers. Then I picked up my coat, walking to the closet to hang it on a wooden hanger.

My plan for the evening was to unpack while I waited for my champagne. Then I'd have a glass, peruse the room service menu and order dinner. Then I'd have another glass and a bath followed by more glasses until the bottle was empty.

There'd be no need for a predawn alarm tomorrow, and maybe if I drank enough, I'd sleep through my body's alarm too.

I carried my suitcase across the room to the drawers and flopped it on the carpet, opening it slowly. The instant the zipper was free, the clothes inside exploded, spilling onto the carpet like they'd been holding their breath during the trip and could finally exhale.

Want a chocolate soufflé or croquembouche? I could whip those up without breaking a sweat. Pack light for a three-day trip? Sorry, wrong girl.

I carefully refolded pajama pants and tank tops before placing them in a drawer. The two pairs of jeans I'd brought plus a black dress—because Christmas dinner might demand a dress—were hung in the closet. And my collection of panties and bras, extra in case of emergency, were safely stowed in another drawer. I took my toiletry case to the bathroom and was about to zip the empty suitcase closed when my phone dinged again. I swiped it off the bed and my heart dropped.

Dad.

"Damn it."

I scrunched up my nose, pacing in front of the door. Should I answer? Decline? The only reason he was calling was because I hadn't shown up at the party tonight. He couldn't know that I'd left California for the holiday, right?

I'd left hours ago. But if one of his minion-spies had been trailing me, he would have known this morning that I'd left the state.

Last year, when I'd threatened to disown him if he didn't call off his hounds, Dad had agreed to no more bodyguards. Without them cataloging my every move, there was no way he could know I was in Montana.

There was only one way to find out.

"Ugh." I hit the green circle. "Hi, Dad."

"Cleo."

Oh boy, he was mad. *Shit.* He said my name in that quiet, ominous tone I'd only heard twice in my life, once after I'd flunked math my junior year and once when I'd gotten caught making out with the neighbor boy in the pool house.

"I'm sorry for missing your party tonight."

"Are you sick?" he asked.

"No."

There was noise in the background, idle chatter and the clinking of glasses, but Dad remained silent.

This was his signature tactic. One he'd perfected in the boardroom and brought home to test on his children. He would wait people out because eventually, the lack of conversation would make the other party break.

And the other party always caved. Always. Why? Because I was the other party. And I spoke up every damn time.

"I love you, Dad, but I can't do another crazy Christmas." It was better this way. I'd just come clean, tell him I'd miss the festivities, and then he wouldn't worry. I'd make it up to him with his favorite strudel when I got back to California.

"So you left to spend it alone in Montana?"

The nagging guilt vanished in a snap. My spine stiffened. "How do you know I am in Montana?"

"We'll expect you home tomorrow. Selene has a big evening planned for Christmas Eve. Then we can enjoy a quiet Christmas morning before the guests arrive in the afternoon."

"You didn't answer my question. How did you know I was in Montana?" I articulated every word.

"Tomorrow, Cleo."

"No." A raging fire spread through my veins. "First, let's pretend like you didn't go against my wishes and betray my trust by having me followed."

"Cleo—"

"Second, let me repeat this so it is inescapably clear. I will not be joining you tomorrow. I've arranged for my gifts to be delivered. Merry Christmas." I ended the call before he could protest, then held the button to power it down before shoving it into my purse.

"Grr." I squeezed my eyes shut and clenched my fists.

Liar. What a goddamn liar!

Dad had promised he wouldn't have me followed. He'd promised. So much for honesty. Had he put a tracking device on my phone? Had one of his henchmen followed me to the airport? I wouldn't put it past him to monitor my credit card activity.

For years, I'd put up with the bodyguards lurking around every corner. I'd humored Dad's safety demands. After what had happened to my mother, I understood his concerns. But I wasn't an eighteen-year-old girl heading off to college. I wasn't twenty-one and staying out too late at night partying with her friends.

I was twenty-eight years old and capable of taking care of myself.

I was capable of planning my own fucking Christmas.

Where is my champagne?

My father and I had been so close once. He'd been my best friend. After Mom had died, it had just been the two of us. We'd clung to one another and become a team. His overprotective tendencies hadn't bothered me then either because I'd been a child.

But we'd drifted apart these past ten years. I'd grown up. Dad had met Selene and the entire dynamic of our home had shifted.

She was twelve years my senior. It was a strange age gap because she wasn't old enough to be my parent and most of the time it had felt like I'd been saddled with a big sister, not a stepmom.

I loved my half-brother, Ray Jr., but I didn't *like* him much. He was as spoiled and selfish as his mother. Last year, he'd thrown a tantrum because I hadn't bought him a gift. Instead, I'd brought pastries and cakes for the entire household to share, doubling up on my brother's favorite éclairs so he wouldn't have to share his dozen.

But who was I to call anyone selfish? Maybe it was just as selfish of me to disappear to Montana instead of spending time with my family. Maybe I was spoiled because rather than confront my father about the spectacle that the holidays had become, I'd taken the coward's way out and disappeared.

Except staying in California hadn't been an option. Dad would have shown up at my doorstep and collected me himself.

Maybe if he ever listened to me, I would have instigated that conversation.

"Like he listened about the security detail," I muttered to the room.

He'd promised, *to my face*, and done whatever he wanted to anyway.

Screw this. I was staying in Montana and having my own Christmas for a change.

No bratty kids complaining because the thousands of dollars in gifts weren't enough. No extravagant parties where I was forced into heels and a cocktail dress as I made small talk with Dad's business associates. No vegan Christmas dinner because my stepmother was on a new diet.

I was in Montana and I was staying.

A knock at the door had me springing into action, salivating for my champagne. I grabbed a twenty from my purse to give as a tip, then ripped the door open. "Thank—"

No.

My stomach dropped to the fuzzy slippers on my feet.

"What the hell are you doing here?"

CHAPTER TWO

AUSTIN

"Get your stuff," I ordered Cleo. The last place I wanted to be two days before Christmas was Montana. Maybe she wanted to escape here for a white Christmas, but sunshine, palm trees and seventy-degree weather suited me just fine. "Let's go."

"Why won't anyone answer my questions?" she asked under her breath, her eyes narrowing at me. "Let's try this again. What. Are. You. Doing. Here?"

"Collecting you." I pushed past her into the room and set my backpack down. Then I walked to the closet, ripping the door open and hauling out her empty suitcase before tossing it on the bed. I pointed toward it as it bounced. "Pack up."

"No." Cleo crossed her arms over her chest, stepping away from the door to let it slam closed. "I'm not leaving, Austin."

"Yes, you are." The sooner the better. The second to last place I wanted to be two days before Christmas was in Cleo's hotel room, beside a bed. "Hustle up."

"No." She huffed. "No, I'm not leaving."

"Damn, but you are difficult."

She jutted out her chin.

The movement shifted the loose waves of her long, brown hair. The color always reminded me of the cocoa buttercream frosting she used on my favorite cupcakes. Her hazel eyes flared brighter, like they always did when she was angry, and the green flecks glowed.

I sucked in a breath, willing my temper and self-control into submission, but all it got me was a deep inhale of her scent. Sweet honey infused with her favorite cinnamon gum. Fuck, I really needed to get out of this hotel room.

There was a reason I avoided Cleo. There was a reason I made sure never to be alone with her in a confined space. Cleo Hillcrest was a beautiful, enchanting, infuriating woman and the daughter of my biggest client.

Cleo Hillcrest was categorically off-limits.

And she hated me to boot. Well, as close to hate as Cleo could come. She was too good, too sweet, to truly hate.

But her brand of hatred was exactly how I preferred things between us. How I'd designed it. As soon as I hauled her home to California, we could go back to the way things had been. Me, pretending like she didn't exist. Her, cursing the day I'd been born.

Harmony.

"This isn't up for debate." I mirrored her stance and jerked my chin to the suitcase. "Pack."

"Unbelievable." She seethed. "I haven't seen you in three months. The last time you spoke to me you criticized my work, my hair and my clothing. Now you're here, ruining my vacation."

I had criticized her, and I'd do it again. I'd walked into Crumbs and she'd been behind the register. She'd given me a smile so sweet it had made my heart skip. So I'd told her that the croissant she'd given me the day before was dry, her hair was looking a little flat and that the flour covering her jeans and T-shirt was an improvement because it made them less boring.

Not the nicest way to say hello but it had erased her sweet smile and the only thing in my heart had been guilt.

I'd planned on apologizing the next time I saw her, but that same day, her father had called to inform me that my job duties were to change. He'd made an agreement with Cleo. No more bodyguards. No more round-the-clock security.

It was all bullshit.

The only deal Ray had made was with me. My team was to ensure Cleo's safety from an unnoticeable distance.

Without Ray's business, my own would suffer. So for the past three months, a member of my team had watched her from afar. It had only been a matter of time before she'd spotted us or caught on to her father's deception, though I'd expected it to happen in California, not Montana.

It was going to be a cluster when we got home. If we got home.

"You have thirty seconds to start packing," I said. "Either you do it yourself, or I'll do it for you."

"I hate you." Her lip curled.

A knock at the door interrupted her snarl.

"Pack." I brushed past her, desperate for some outside air, and flung the door open. A kid, probably eighteen, greeted me with a smile. It dropped when he met my icy glare.

"Oh, uh . . . sorry." His eyes darted to a slip of paper on the tray he was carrying. "I'm looking for a Ms. Hillcrest. This says room four-ten."

"I'm here." Cleo appeared at my side, jabbing me in the ribs with her elbow, muttering, "Move."

I swallowed a grunt. Damn, she had sharp elbows.

"Can you send up another bottle?" Cleo asked the kid, taking the ice bucket and champagne off the tray. "I'm going to need two."

"And another glass, ma'am?"

"No." She snatched the single flute he'd brought and shot me a glare. "He's leaving."

The kid's gaze lifted to my face and I nodded at the hallway for him to get lost.

He followed orders, even the nonverbal kind, much better than the stubborn woman who marched back inside the room.

"I'm not leaving," she declared, setting the champagne on the closest nightstand. "I came here for a vacation and to celebrate Christmas on my own terms. I'm not spending another inane, material, superficial holiday with my family."

Cleo hauled the green bottle from the bucket, peeling off the foil and yanking away the muselet. Then she pressed her thumbs against the cork, bracing for the pop. Except the cork didn't budge. Her cheeks reddened and her lips pursed as she gripped the bottle in one hand and attempted to shimmy and wiggle out the cork with the other. Still, it didn't budge.

I growled and stepped close, ripping the bottle from her hands.

"Hey. Give that back." She swiped for it, but I spun and blocked her with my shoulder.

With a twist and a tug, the cork popped free. "Here."

She took the bottle back and stomped—as well as a person could stomp in a pair of fluffy white slippers—to the flute, pouring it until the fizz reached the brim. "My father promised me there'd be no more security. He promised."

"That's between the two of you."

She gulped the entire glass of champagne and immediately refilled it. "How long? Tell me the truth. How long have you been following me?"

Ray had asked me not to tell Cleo about our agreement. But the look in her eyes, the desperation for someone to be honest with her, broke my resolve. "We never stopped."

Her shoulders fell.

I hated being the one to put the sad look on her face. Just like I hated being the one to erase her smiles. But I was on the clock here and things would be easier once she was home and far, far away from me.

This entire trip was so out of character for her. Cleo loved routine more than any person I knew. It made it ridiculously easy to protect her. Up at four. To the bakery by five. Work until close, then she drove home, lights out by eight.

Ray hadn't believed me when I'd called him this morning and told him that his daughter had just boarded a plane, final destination Montana.

He'd cussed me up one side and down the other, but we hadn't been monitoring her credit cards. He'd told us to stop three months ago, wanting to give her at least that much autonomy. So much for her independence. As of today, every movement Cleo made, every purchase, was to be tracked by my team. Anything suspicious was to be reported to him immediately.

Like a trip to Montana for Christmas.

Three hours after he'd hung up on me, I'd been sent

instructions to *get my ass to the airport,* board his private plane and retrieve his daughter.

The jet was parked and waiting at the Quincy airport to take us home.

"Drink your champagne. Then we'll go."

"No." Her voice was calm and flat. Resolute, but polite. "I'm sorry you came all this way for no reason, Austin, but I'm not leaving."

Shit. Cleo rarely dug her heels in, but when she did, she planted them hard and deep.

If she didn't leave, there was a good chance I'd get fired. Ray was normally a fair man to work for, but where his daughter was concerned, the man wouldn't see reason.

Which was probably why Cleo hadn't told him about this vacation in the first place.

Ray owned a cybersecurity company that had boomed over the past thirty years. Mirror Networks was valued at over fifteen billion dollars, and as the founder and CEO, Ray had a level of wealth that was impossible for me to comprehend.

He'd had a physical security company on his payroll for over twenty years. The company before mine had been his long-time provider, but when one of the bodyguards had hit on Cleo and made her uncomfortable, he'd terminated the contract immediately, as any father should.

I would have done the same.

That was four years ago and since, he'd been with my company, Garrison. I'd been a startup at the time and busted my ass to prove myself to the man. It had been the hardest four years of my damn life—and not because of Ray.

Because of Cleo.

The good thing was, Ray didn't seem to care that Cleo hated me. As long as I kept her safe, I stayed in his good graces and his monthly payment hit my bank account on the first.

But if I went home alone, he'd terminate our contract.

The guys who worked for me had families. They needed a steady paycheck and if I lost Ray, it would take me years to replace that income, especially if he spread word around LA that I'd left his daughter in an unsafe situation.

So Cleo had to come home, whether she wanted to or not.

"The jet is waiting at the airport," I told her.

"Great." She threw out a hand toward the door. "Don't miss your ride. I'll be back after Christmas."

"Cleo—"

"And think, you won't have to hide out anymore. The jig is up. When I get home, you can come into the bakery and tell me all about how much you hate my food."

Son of a bitch. There was hurt in her voice, and it was like a knife to the heart. I'd done that. I'd wounded her with my muttered critiques and blatant dismissal of anything she created.

But it was for the best. We came from different worlds.

Eventually, this feeling would go away and she'd be just another client.

"Why are you so stuck on staying?" I asked. "Is this really what you want? Christmas alone in a hotel room?"

"Yes, it is."

"Why?" Christmas was one of my favorite holidays. Spending a day with my family was something I looked forward to all year long, and it was the one day of the year that I made sure I had off.

"The entire day is just one big show."

"And you're too spoiled and selfish to put up with it for a day." It was overly harsh, but maybe if I pissed her off, she'd be less likely to stay.

"Get out." The snarl returned. "Get. Out. Now."

"Pack your things. We're going home."

"No! I'm not leaving!" Her voice shook. "I'm an adult. I'm a grown woman. If I want to take a vacation for Christmas, I have every right. I don't have to explain myself to my father. Or to you."

"You're right." I nodded. "But I'm still taking you home."

"How much is my father paying you to babysit me?"

"We're not babysitting you." I scowled. "We're doing our best to keep you safe."

She knew just how much I hated the word *babysitter*. She threw it in my face when she was particularly angry. I was here to protect her. I'd put my life on the line to keep hers safe. To compare me to a teenage babysitter was the ultimate insult.

"Pack." I pointed to the suitcase.

Cleo rolled her eyes and drained the champagne flute dry. Then she turned, filling it once more. At this rate, the bottle would be empty within ten minutes. Maybe if she was drunk, she'd be easier to convince.

"Protecting me from what?" she asked. "I'm not in danger. Especially here. Unless you think the bellboy might try and smile me to death."

"There are evil people in this world, Cleo. Your father is doing what he thinks is best."

"He's unilaterally making decisions for my life. And I'm well aware there are evil people in this world, so please save me the lecture."

Christ. Why had I thought this would be an easy day? The minute I'd been told Cleo was en route to the airport, I should have expected this showdown.

I rubbed the back of my neck as she gulped more champagne. Just as her glass emptied, a knock sounded at the door. I took a step to answer it, but she shot me a glare and tried to beat me to the knob. She wasn't fast enough. I checked the peephole, seeing the kid from earlier, and opened the door.

"Hi." She sidestepped me, smiling at the kid. Then she slipped a twenty-dollar bill from her pocket, trading him the cash for the fresh bottle. "Thank you."

"Have a good night, Ms. Hillcrest." He bowed, refusing to look my way, then closed the door.

Cleo turned and shoved the champagne into my gut. "Make yourself useful."

Fuck, this woman made me crazy.

I opened her bottle as she marched to the chest of drawers and flung one open.

Finally. She was packing.

A pair of crimson silk pajama shorts and a matching top floated through the air as she tossed them over her shoulder and onto the bed. I expected more to follow, but she stood, snatched them up, cast a sneer at the suitcase and yanked the fresh bottle of champagne from my grip. Then she marched to the bathroom, kicking the door closed and flipping the lock.

"Oh for fuck's sake," I muttered. "Seriously?"

The only response was a string of muffled noises from the other side of the door.

I dug the phone from my pocket and pulled up Ray's name, ready to dial. But before I could bring myself to call and give him an update, I shut the screen off and tucked the phone away.

Ray's primary concern was his family's safety. I didn't fault the guy for it. After what had happened to his wife, I understood why he went overboard.

His first wife and Cleo's mother, Janet, had been murdered.

Ray had amassed a fortune while Cleo had been a

baby. Though according to his long-time assistant, Ray and Janet had lived humbly. Apparently, it was night and day compared to the lavish lifestyle Ray had bestowed upon his second wife, Selene.

Years ago, when Cleo had just been a little girl, Ray had fired a guy for misconduct. That employee had then made threats not only against Ray, but also against Janet and Cleo as well. Ray hadn't thought much of it, chalking it up to a disgruntled former employee who was mouthing off and would eventually disappear.

He'd been wrong. Terribly wrong. And his wife had paid for it with her life.

Janet had left home to run an errand one day. Ray had been at work. Cleo had been in preschool. The guy had stopped Janet six blocks from home and shot her twice in the heart.

Since, Ray had taken security to the extreme.

What man in his shoes wouldn't? I understood the motives for his over-the-top measures. Hell, many famous singers and actors and sports stars didn't have the level of security Ray required for Cleo. But at the same time, I understood Cleo's need for freedom. There had to be a balance. A compromise. Only it wasn't my job to broker the arrangement.

My job was simply to get Cleo home.

The door to the bathroom opened and she walked out, her chin held high. She carried her champagne to the nightstand and set it down beside the empty bottle, then swiped up a binder near the lamp, flipping it open as she plopped onto the edge of the bed.

I blinked. Twice. Not because she was ignoring me. But because my mind was blank. My tongue was three sizes too big and my eyes didn't know where to look first.

Her legs? No, her arms. Her chest. No, definitely her legs.

There was a lot of skin on display, from the scalloped hem of her sleep shorts all the way down toned thighs and trim calves to her dainty ankles. Her delectable feet were hidden by those slippers.

I forced my eyes up and they landed on the smooth line of her neck. She'd twisted her hair up and a dark tendril curled behind the shell of her ear. She wore no jewelry, not even the diamond studs that were her favorite because they'd been Janet's. I'd overheard her tell that to Brynne at the bakery one day, two years ago.

I stared at the lobes of her naked ears, refusing to let my gaze drop beyond her neck. Because below her collarbones, her top was nothing more than a scrap of silk. A cropped top that showed a hint of midriff. The spaghetti straps left her arms and shoulders bare. And the wide V-neck plunged much, much too low.

Leave. Get out. My mind screamed for me to walk out the door because this was my client's daughter, but my body was fighting for the other team. The team that wanted me to cross the room, pull Cleo into my arms and find out if she tasted as sweet as her confections.

29

I had to get the fuck out of this room.

Cleo had twenty-four-seven security, but there was a reason why I always assigned her to a member of my team, why I didn't monitor her personally. I didn't trust myself. When she was in the room, I wasn't aware of my surroundings. I was aware of her. Only her.

At thirty-three years old, I'd never met a person who could block out the world.

Until Cleo.

And damn it, I couldn't exactly haul her out of here wearing those skimpy pajamas. "I'll give you one night. One. Then we're leaving in the morning."

"Whatever." She sipped her champagne and studied the room service menu. She flipped the page and leaned forward to study the text. The gap at the front of her top loosened, barely covering those gorgeous breasts. Her nipples peaked through the thin fabric.

Fuck me.

Without another word, I strode to the door, flinging it open at the same time I swiped my backpack from the floor. The echo of the door's slam followed me as I marched down the hallway to the elevator. I punched the down arrow three times, practically jumping in once it arrived.

When I reached the lobby, I found a quiet corner beside the Christmas tree and called the pilot, giving him the go-ahead to return to California alone. He offered to spend the night, but there was no reason for us all to be stuck in Montana before Christmas. I'd get a ticket with Cleo and we'd fly back commercial in the morning.

I slumped forward in the chair, my backpack resting at my feet, and closed my eyes before pinching the bridge of my nose. Goddamn it. Goddamn this trip. Goddamn Ray. Avoiding him was futile so I dialed his number.

He didn't answer.

Why would he? He and Selene were hosting one of their annual Christmas-week *soirees* and had a house full of rich people. All he cared about was that Cleo was safe and would be home promptly. What he didn't know tonight wouldn't kill him.

I stood and took in the lobby, assessing exits and entrances. Casing a place had become habit over my career. The inn was cozy and classy without being stuffy. If not for the snow, it would be the perfect holiday getaway. A big improvement over the party Cleo was avoiding at her father's house.

If I were wearing her slippers, I would have skipped town too. Not that I'd admit that to her.

I was the hired help and no one, especially Ray, gave a shit about my opinion.

Tomorrow, I'd get Cleo to California. She'd be fully clothed and those pajamas a distant memory. Then I'd go back to my life and she'd go back to hers. The only contact I'd have with Cleo would be the weekly report that crossed my desk from the team assigned to her detail.

Maybe one of these days she'd get a serious boyfriend

who lasted longer than a month and this attraction I had for her would fizzle out. I mean, it hadn't in four years, but eventually it had to fade, right?

I raked a hand through my hair and crossed the lobby for the front desk. At least I'd thought to bring a bag, not that it had much other than my laptop, charging cords and a bottle of aspirin.

The young woman standing behind the counter smiled as I approached. She hadn't been at the desk earlier when I'd entered the lobby. I'd been prepared to deliver some bullshit line about being Cleo's boyfriend here to surprise her for Christmas, but then I'd seen the bellboy set down a tray with one glass and a bottle of champagne in a bucket of ice.

Cleo loved champagne so on a hunch, I'd stolen a glance at the room receipt. Sure enough, her name had been on the ticket beside the room number 410.

"Good evening, sir," *Eloise*, her name tag read, greeted. "How can I help you?"

I dug my wallet from my jeans pocket. "I'd like a room, please."

Her smile fell.

My stomach plummeted. Oh hell.

"I'm so sorry, sir, but we're sold out for the week. Christmas and all."

"Of course," I muttered through gritted teeth.

Fucking Montana.

CHAPTER THREE

CLEO

"He can go to hell," I muttered to the empty room.

Who the hell did he think he was, following me here and ordering me around like I was a child? I was an adult and didn't need a babysitter.

"One night?" I scoffed. "I'm not leaving. This is my vacation. Mine. This is my Christmas."

I flew off the bed, too antsy to sit still, and paced the room.

After Austin had left, I'd made considerable progress drinking the second bottle of champagne. Half a flute and it would be gone. My head was fuzzy. My limbs were loose and warm. My stomach growled and I hiccupped, staring at the door, willing my room service to appear. I was starving, having only eaten airplane pretzels for lunch, and food would help soak up some of the alcohol.

I didn't need a raging hangover if I had to travel home

tomorrow, and it was very likely I would be traveling.

Austin Myles usually got his way.

I wouldn't put it past him to toss me over his shoulder and cart me out of here if he so desired.

Once upon a time, I'd dreamed of being carried off by Austin, willingly, without a kick or a scream. When my father had hired his company to provide physical security for the family, I'd taken one look at Austin—at his midnight hair and hypnotic eyes—and boom. *Hello, crush.* That's all it was. A teensy, tiny, enormous crush.

But I'd hid it well. Not a soul on earth knew how I felt about Austin and I'd take my itty-bitty crush to the grave.

When he'd first started working for us, my father had insisted Austin personally see to my protection. Dad had been paranoid that I was at risk ever since I'd opened Crumbs. From who was a mystery, but Dad wasn't much for reason when it came to his daughter.

So Austin had done a full assessment of my life. He'd been all business, focusing on assessing security at the bakery and at my home. It had been cute, the way he'd carried a notebook around, jotting down notes about access points and breach potential—if one could call a six foot three, muscled heartthrob *cute.*

After Austin's inspection, he'd deemed my home and workplace safe enough but in need of improvement. I'd owned the bakery for a year by that point and had never had a problem, but that hadn't stopped him from installing a new locking system on the rear entrance as well as an entire video surveillance system. There was an alarm fob on my keychain. A can of pepper spray in my nightstand.

The system and safeguards should have been enough, but Dad had still insisted on a bodyguard. It had been Austin in the early days. He'd sit at a corner table in the bakery, working on his laptop in silence, paying me next to no attention. Though I had no doubt that if a customer had so much as raised a voice he would have come to my rescue.

Apparently, the only person allowed to criticize me or my baked goods was Austin himself.

Then one day, it hadn't been Austin who'd shown up at my house at five in the morning to escort me to work. It had been one of his team members. And the days when I'd glimpsed Austin had become fewer and farther between.

At first, I'd worried that he suspected my crush. That he thought of me as that silly girl six years his junior. Then his true colors had shown. The reason Austin avoided me like the mall on Black Friday was because he didn't like me.

He'd made that perfectly clear three months ago when he'd come to the bakery and insulted me.

That was the day I'd called my father and said enough. No more bodyguards. No more Austin. My foolish heart had been bruised one too many times.

Dad had promised to lighten up security. How stupid was I to have believed him?

Where had Austin and his team been lurking? Had

they stayed outside the bakery all day long? Did he have someone stationed undercover? I had plenty of regulars at the bakery, a couple in particular that might fit in Austin's crew. Tall. Broad. Muscled. Brynne always made sure to alert me whenever there was a hot guy on the premises.

So how had they been watching me? Had they hacked my surveillance system? How had they known I'd come to Montana? The assholes were probably monitoring my credit cards. *Bastards*. I wouldn't put it past my father. Or Austin. With his resources, I doubted there was much I could hide.

Garrison, Austin's firm, wasn't the biggest private security company in Los Angeles, not by a long shot. But his was one of the fastest-growing firms with the best reputation.

Austin was known for his risk-assessment skills. Word on the street was—because heaven forbid the man actually talk to me—Austin preferred to take jobs with the entrepreneurial wealthy. He didn't like the drama and spotlight that came with celebrities. His clientele consisted of people like my father, those who stayed under the radar but who made enough money that some whacko might try to kidnap their kids and ask for ransom.

Or kill their loved ones.

Dad's motives, though ridiculous at times, were coming from a good place. He was terrified to lose me, like he had Mom.

But there had to be a limit, right? My father's fears

wouldn't hold me prisoner any longer. I was perfectly safe in Montana for three days. When Austin showed up in the morning to escort me home, I was telling him no.

"No." I practiced the word. Easy.

"No." Super easy. I could definitely tell Austin no, with or without liquid courage flooding my veins. I'd done it tonight. I'd do it again tomorrow.

My stomach churned and not from the champagne. Today's show of stubbornness had been an anomaly. And who was I kidding? Telling Austin no was nearly impossible. It was a miracle I'd managed to delay him tonight.

It was his eyes. Those coffee-brown eyes swallowed me whole. I was powerless against them. Maybe tomorrow I'd just avoid eye contact. It would probably be best if I avoided all of his face, period. There wasn't a feature I didn't adore, from the strong line of his nose to his supple lips to his square jaw and high cheekbones.

At least he'd shaved the beard he'd grown last year. Had he shown up in Montana with the beard, I'd be on an airplane instead of waiting for room service.

I'd only seen it once but the image of his sculpted jaw covered in perfectly groomed, dark hair was committed to memory. Austin had walked into the bakery after I'd gotten into an, erm . . . altercation with the guy on duty. The weather had been unseasonably warm and the air conditioner had quit, so I'd propped the back door open to get some air circulating and combat the heat from the ovens.

Well, the guy on duty hadn't liked having the door open. I'd told him tough luck. He'd called in his boss.

In true Austin fashion, he'd gotten his way. I'd closed the door, blaming my moment of weakness on the beard.

Thankfully, it was gone now. Austin was back to his usual clean-cut self. Dark jeans, polished boots and a starched, long-sleeved button-up. Though today, he'd rolled the sleeves up his forearms, revealing the dusting of dark hair.

Just once, I wanted to see him smile. I couldn't think of a time I'd seen his teeth. But why would he smile at me? He hated me as much as I pretended to hate him.

My minuscule, insignificant, harmless crush was surprisingly resilient. No matter how many times he flustered or frustrated me, the damn thing wouldn't die.

Because Austin Myles was a dream.

He was a good man. He loved his mother—I'd overheard him talking to her on the phone twice and the adoration and love in his voice had brought tears to my eyes. His employees looked up to him, respected and appreciated his steady leadership. He carried an air of authority and confidence, but he didn't use his charisma to intimidate or make others feel insecure. He was levelheaded. Smart. He held the door open for others and let the elderly cut in line.

My life would be easier if I hated him like he hated me.

Why did he dislike me so? Did he really think I was

spoiled and selfish? Austin wasn't rude to anyone except me. What was it about my personality that put him on edge?

Well, screw him. I was nice. I was likable. I was a good baker. And he was ruining my Christmas.

A surge of anger raced through my body and I closed my eyes, holding it tight. I'd need it tomorrow because I wasn't going home. Call me selfish. Call me spoiled. Call me a brat. I was staying in Montana for three days, whether Austin liked it or not.

"So there." I stomped my slippered foot.

I'd have to call and explain to my father that it wasn't Austin's fault. Dad would probably fire him otherwise. But no matter how much they pushed, I wasn't backing down. If I did, I'd lose a lot more than this getaway.

A knock sounded at the door.

"Yessss. Food." I didn't bother checking the peephole. Again. I was really going to have to work on that. Because there he was, the star of my fantasies, here to ruin Christmas once more. "You said I got one night. Go away."

Austin pushed his way past me, sending a waft of his sexy, spicy cologne straight to my nostrils.

I inhaled and held it in. God, I was pathetic.

"They're out of rooms," he said, walking around the end of the bed to the side closest to the window, barely giving me a glance as he set his backpack beside the dresser. He took the phone from his pocket and deposited it on the nightstand. Next came the wallet from his jeans pocket.

As he moved, my gaze wandered down his spine, past his belt and to his scrumptious behind—when a man had an ass that perfect, any woman two bottles of champagne into the night would look.

Austin gripped the sides of his shirt and yanked it free from the waist of his jeans.

My mouth watered. Then the two brain cells still functioning in my hazy stupor tuned into what was happening here. Austin was making himself comfortable. "Oh, no. No. No. No. No. No. You can't stay in here."

"They're out of rooms," he repeated.

"Then find another hotel!" My hands flew in the air as I shrieked. There was no way I could sleep in the same room—and bed—as Austin Myles.

"There is one other hotel in Quincy, Montana, and a bed-and-breakfast. And they're all sold out."

"Then go to another town."

He scowled. "The nearest town is fifty miles away. Trust me, I asked."

Oh, God. This wasn't happening. We could not share a bed. What if I fell asleep and tried to cuddle with him? Or worse, what if my hands wandered and I groped him while unconscious?

"Then go home. Take the plane. I'll call my father and tell him I refused to come home. I'll make sure he knows that it was my decision and—"

"Cleo, calm down." Austin held up a hand. "It's one night. Would you mind just putting something on?"

I glanced down at myself and a crimson wave of shame spread across my skin. I imagined the color was about the same as my silk pajamas.

I'd put them on earlier to scare Austin off. It had worked. Except now it was painfully obvious that my nipples were pebbled and there was a lot of skin showing.

My arms banded around my chest and I rushed to my drawers, finding a cream sweater and pulling it over my head. The moment it was on, draping midthigh, Austin's shoulders relaxed away from his ears.

Really? Were my nipples that horrific? *Ugh*. Why did I have to crush on such a jackass?

Another knock came at the door and I turned, ready to collect my dinner, but in a flash Austin vaulted over the bed and was yanking me away from the door.

"Peephole." He pointed to the circle.

I pointed to the handle. "Room service."

He frowned and opened the door, barely cracking it until he could assess who was on the other side.

"Seriously," I muttered.

Austin opened the door further, not before shooting me a scowl, and waved the same bellboy from earlier inside.

I rushed to my purse, taking out another twenty because this kid had earned it tonight. "Thank you."

He nodded and his smile widened as I handed over his

tip. "Just roll the cart into the hallway when you're done and I'll come collect it later tonight. Have a good night, ma'am."

"You too."

The moment he pulled the door closed, Austin flipped the deadbolt and secured the chain.

"Paranoid much?" I lifted the metal lid on my plate and the smell of french fries and a cheeseburger filled the room.

Whoa. The Eloise Inn didn't mess around. They'd sent an entire basket of fries with nacho cheese on the side, and the burger was bigger than my face.

Austin's gaze zeroed in on my food.

Good. Maybe if he was hungry enough, he'd go somewhere else to find food. Like West Hollywood.

His stomach growled, but he didn't make a move to leave. The man would probably starve himself rather than give up and leave this room and concede me a victory. The stubborn mule.

There went the growl again. It echoed in the room like a hungry lion trapped in the cage that was his flat stomach.

Damn it. Couldn't he shut that animal up? It growled again and my nerves began to falter. My inner nurturer was starting to break out in hives as the growling continued. The overwhelming urge to feed people, to bring them joy through sugar, carbohydrates and fat, was engrained deep in my soul.

Damn it, again.

"Would you like to share? I won't eat all of this myself," I muttered. Or he could call and order his own cheeseburger. Maybe I should have just tossed the binder in his face.

"I'm good to share." Austin's dark eyes met mine and he gave me a small smile. There were no teeth showing but it was a smile, nonetheless. "Thanks."

My crush flared like a skin rash immune to hydrocortisone cream.

Hopeless. I was hopeless.

I turned my attention to the meal, dividing it between the plate and basket. "Would you like some champagne?" Not that there was much left.

"No." He took the plate I offered and returned to his side of the bed, propping himself up against some pillows.

"Water?" I walked to the minifridge and took out a bottle for myself.

"Please."

I retrieved another, then sat on the bed, mirroring his posture, and popped a fry into my mouth.

He did the same.

Next I went for the burger.

Austin kept eating fries.

Five bites in—there was nothing else to do but count—I wanted to hide in the bathtub to eat. Awkward wasn't a strong enough word for this.

We didn't look at one another. We didn't speak. But it was impossible to ignore, especially in my getting-drunkerby-the-second state, every one of Austin's movements. I could feel the heat radiating off his body, and his broad shoulders took up half the bed, putting us much, much too close. His legs were so long that even dangling off the edge, I knew he'd have to sleep at a slight diagonal to fit.

There would be touching.

Oh, sweet Jesus, we were going to touch. It was terrifying, yet exhilarating. If my crush were a small rash, it would probably be a full-body breakout by morning.

What was he going to wear? Would he strip down to boxers? A shirtless Austin would be one hell of a Christmas present, but knowing Austin, he'd sleep on the floor, fully clothed with a scowl aimed my way all night long.

"It's snowing." Austin shot a glare at the window.

Outside, illuminated by the streetlamps, fat clumps of snow floated through the air like icy feathers. "Isn't it pretty?"

He turned to me, his face screwed up in horror like I'd just told him Santa Claus wasn't real.

I waved him off and lifted my basket. "More fries?"

"No." Austin shook his head and returned his gaze to the window. "Why couldn't you have run away in the summer?"

"Excuse me?" My spine stiffened. "I'm not a child. I didn't run away. I went on a *vacation*."

"That's not what I mean."

"Then what do you mean?" I swung my legs off the

bed and took my basket to the cart, setting it down with too much force.

"You know."

"Obviously, I don't," I grumbled, reaching for my drink. In this room, the champagne was the only thing on my side. And my slippers.

"What I mean is . . . you're calm," Austin explained. "Levelheaded."

"Predictable."

"Yes."

"Boring," I mumbled before taking a long gulp.

"I didn't say that."

He didn't have to. A lot of people thought that my life should be more exciting. My father was a billionaire. Dad would give me anything in the world if it was at his disposal, no questions asked. I didn't travel the world. I didn't spend frivolously. My idea of an exciting Friday night was experimenting with pastry recipes.

"I get it," I said. "This isn't the type of thing I normally do and it's taken everyone off guard. Cleo has a mind of her own. Surprise."

I swiped the TV remote from the dresser and turned it on. The generic music from the guide channel filled the room as I returned to my side of the bed, taking care to sit as close to the edge as possible.

The Hallmark Channel was my favorite this time of year because cheesy holiday romances made me smile. I found it in the guide, punched in the number and the minute the channel changed, a couple dry humping filled the screen.

Kill me now.

Austin swiped the remote from my hand and didn't miss a beat as he found a sports show. It was the one and only time I wouldn't complain about basketball.

"Uh . . . who's watching the store?" he asked, crossing his arms over his chest. He was also hovering close to his edge of the bed.

"Brynne."

He hummed, his eyes fixed on the screen.

I did my best to follow the game, but as the ball moved from one end of the court to the other, the champagne soaked into my blood, making me sleepy. Before I could crash, I forced myself off the bed and into the bathroom, where I washed my face and brushed my teeth. Then I braced my hands by the sink and met my reflection in the mirror.

One night.

You can make it one night.

Then I'd sit Austin down, sans champagne, and calmly explain to him that I needed this trip. He'd go home and I'd have two blissful nights alone in my hotel room.

I slathered on my night cream, then took off the sweater I'd pulled on because there was no way I was sleeping in merino wool, then eased out of the bathroom.

Austin's eyes snapped to me the second the door

opened. He'd taken the food cart and my champagne bottles and bucket to the hallway but was back on his side of the bed.

I kept my chin high and walked to the bed, turning down the covers and sliding beneath. Then I stretched an arm to the lamp and turned it off. "Goodnight, Austin."

"Goodnight, Cleo." He shifted, kicking off his boots.

My eyes darted to his socks as he lifted his feet onto the bed. "Are those pizza socks?"

"Yeah," he muttered, flipping off the light on his side of the room. "My mom bought them for me."

Heart. Melt.

He wore dorky socks because they were a gift from his mother.

I shifted onto my other side to face him. "I'm sorry you had to come here. That wasn't my intention."

He looked down at me and his gaze softened. "I know."

If he knew, then why was he so angry? Why did I irritate him so much?

"Why do you hate me?" I whispered, instantly regretting the words and the two bottles of champagne that had given me the courage to blurt them. Partially drunk was out the window. Clearly, I was fucking wasted. But I didn't take back my question. I stared up at him, hoping he'd answer.

"It's easier."

Easier?

Austin's gaze drifted to my lips. He stared at them like . . . wait, did he want to kiss me? Because I would be totally okay with that. But why would he want to kiss me? Austin didn't like me that way. Or any way.

I opened my mouth to ask what he was talking about, but in a flash, he was gone.

He pulled his boots on faster than any man in the history of boot-wearing men and picked up his phone and wallet. Those were shoved in his pockets as he strode around the bed and toward the door.

I propped up on an elbow, my eyes tracking his every step. "Where are you going?"

He hesitated at the door, glancing over his shoulder. "I'm going to go scope out the place."

"Scope it out?" A laugh escaped. "We're in Montana."

His expression hardened.

This look, I knew well.

It was the one he gave me whenever I offered him something from the bakery. It was the one he favored whenever I protested a security measure. It was the look he gave me whenever I smiled his way.

"Yes, Cleo, we're in Montana," he clipped. "And whose fault is that?"

Before I could respond, he was out the door. And for the first time all night, I just wanted to go home.

CHAPTER FOUR

CLEO

Someone was pounding a drum in the room next door. A really loud, extremely painful drum.

No. Wait. That was just my pulse.

"Fuck you, champagne," I groaned, squeezing my eyes shut and hoping this headache would disappear.

I limited myself to one bottle. Always. One bottle and then I switched to water. I'd had that rule since my best friend from college had gotten married and I'd chugged champagne at the reception like it was the maid of honor's duty to test that all bottles were carbonated.

The one-bottle rule hadn't even crossed my mind last night, thanks to Austin, but if I survived today, I'd never forget again.

I kicked at the covers, trying desperately to unwrap the sheets twined around my legs. When they finally touched air, I swung them over the edge of the bed and—

So that was why my feet were so hot. I'd slept with my slippers on.

My stomach pitched as I sat up, my eyes still closed. I sucked in a deep breath and forced myself to my shaking legs.

Okay. Not bad. I was dizzy but didn't have the urge to vomit. If I could beat this headache, I just might survive.

I took one step and didn't wobble. Win. Except on step number two, everything fell to pieces. The world spun, flipping upside down as my foot caught on something on the floor.

A very large, very angry man sleeping on the floor.

This is going to hurt. I braced, ready for impact, but I didn't collide with the carpet. No, I hit a wall of muscle. A wall that belonged to a very large, very angry man who'd been sleeping on the floor.

"What the fuck?" Austin caught me against his chest, wrapping his arms around me to slow my fall.

"Shh." I patted his chest, working my way up until I felt the softness of his lips. Then I pressed in, sucking in some air as I sat sprawled across his lap.

My eyes, which had somehow stayed closed during the fiasco, cracked open. The dim light that peeked through the slit in the curtains might as well have been high-beam headlights for how they assaulted my irises and amplified the agony in my skull. It hurt so badly, my hands flew to my temples.

"Cleo—"

"Shh," I hissed, louder this time.

On any normal day, I would have appreciated the fact that I was sitting on Austin's lap. That I'd just touched his lips. I would have memorized the bulk of his thighs and the feel of his strong arms. But today, I was seconds from death, and survival was the only thing on my mind. I squirmed out of his hold, and rather than try to stand, I crawled to the bathroom.

Merry Christmas Eve, Cleo.

This was the most humiliating moment of my life and I didn't have it in me to give two flying fucks.

When my palms hit the tile, I moaned as the cool marble calmed my too-hot skin. When my knees crossed the threshold, I gave up and curled into the fetal position, soaking in the chill.

"What are you doing?"

"Shh." I winced and plugged my ears. How many times did a woman have to tell a man to shush before he listened?

"It's four o'clock in the morning."

Austin was scowling. I didn't need to see it because I heard it in his voice.

"It's three in California." My throat burned as I spoke. Why was he even asking? Austin knew my schedule. I arrived at the bakery by five to prep before my drive-up window opened at six. And hangover be damned, my body's alarm clock was blaring.

Okay. Off the floor.

I inhaled some oxygen, then uncurled, deciding maybe my stomach wasn't as steady as I'd initially suspected. I managed to get myself up to a seat and leaned against the wall.

"Are you all right?"

"No." I shook my head, then raised a hand to wave him off.

"Do you want me to shut the door?"

I nodded and pulled my legs into my chest, so they were out of his way. Then he eased it closed, leaving me in the pitch-black bathroom.

Beyond the door, Austin shuffled around the room and it sounded like he plopped down in bed. If it was only four, that meant he'd slept for a little over three hours.

On. The. Floor.

And he called me predictable.

I wasn't sure where he'd disappeared to last night. After an hour of waiting for him to return from *scoping out the place*, I'd drifted off. But because I was a light sleeper, I'd awoken when he'd returned to the room after midnight. I hadn't realized or noticed when he'd snatched a room key, but the click of the lock had startled me out of my drunken slumber. Austin had disappeared into the bathroom and I'd passed out before he'd emerged.

My mouth was dry. My body ached. I stifled a groan. What I needed was water, Advil, caffeine and calories—in that order.

The first two were easy enough to find in the bathroom, even with the lights off. After chugging three of the tiny room glasses and drowning just as many painkillers, I fumbled around until I located my toothbrush. Now all I had to do was find caffeine and calories.

With a fortifying breath, I tiptoed out of the bathroom. Austin was facedown on the bed, fully clothed and sleeping on top of the comforter. I silently walked to the drawers, sliding one open and taking out a bra, sweater and a pair of jeans.

"What are you doing?" Austin asked, not moving as he spoke.

"I need coffee."

He grumbled something into his pillow, then pushed up from the mattress. "Give me a minute."

"No!" Ouch. *Too loud, Cleo.* "Stay. Sleep."

Miraculously, the man didn't argue. He simply buried his face in the pillow.

During last night's reconnaissance mission, he must have deemed Quincy safe. *Shocker.*

I returned to the blissfully dark bathroom and dressed quickly, then found my shoes and picked them up along with some cash from my purse and a room card from the dresser. Even though I knew Austin wasn't asleep, I slipped from the room without a word.

The air in the hallway was warm and smelled like Christmas. Thankfully, the smell didn't make me want to hurl. I made my way to the elevator, my head pounding in rhythm with each step, and when I pushed the button, the ding was earsplitting. When I reached the lobby, the scent of coffee filled my nose and I practically jogged toward the front desk.

The young man stationed behind it did a double take when he saw me coming, then checked his watch. "Morning."

"I need coffee."

He must have sensed my desperation because he hopped off his stool and waved for me to follow. He also didn't speak—*God bless Montanans.*

The front desk was an island in the grand lobby and behind it were two doors. One I assumed was to an office. The other, the door he held for me, opened to an enormous kitchen.

The lights were bright and reflected off the stainless-steel prep table and appliances, but I squinted, my nose leading the way. In the corner of the room, the coffee maker beckoned.

The guy plucked a white, ceramic mug from a tray on the clean side of the dishwasher—we had the same brand at the bakery—then went to the industrial pot and filled my mug nearly to the brim.

"Ice cube?"

I nodded as he went to the ice machine, using the metal scoop to drop two ice cubes into the mug.

"You've done this before."

He grinned and handed me the mug. "Hangovers are a bitch."

"Thank you." The first sip was hot, but the ice cubes helped.

"Ibuprofen?"

I shook my head and gulped more. "I took some already."

"I'm going to leave you here and get back to my post. Drink as much as you'd like."

"Thank you."

He winked before walking out, leaving me in the quiet kitchen.

After two cups, the pain was manageable. I refilled my mug once more, then returned to the lobby.

"Better?" he asked, turning as I pushed through the door.

"Much. Add some food, and you'll have saved my life."

He chuckled and held out his hand. "I'm Mateo."

"Cleo."

"Nice to meet you."

"Likewise." I smiled. "Yesterday, the manager—"

"Eloise. My sister."

Of course, he was one of the Edens. I hadn't noticed the resemblance earlier, but now the similarities in their eyes and the classic shape of their noses were evident. Mateo's smile wasn't sweet like Eloise's, but it was youthful and handsome. I suspected he put that charming smile to good use on the weekends for girls younger than me.

"Eloise said something about a coffee shop. Run by another sister."

"Lyla. She owns the coffee shop, but . . ."

"Don't say it."

He glanced at the clock on his computer screen. "She doesn't open until six thirty."

"Damn." My hands were shaky and with all that coffee sitting in my stomach, I'd be a jittery mess by five.

What I really needed was some dough. Something to knead and work and use to burn off this hangover. If I were at home, I'd make some sort of jelly-filled pastry. Or cinnamon rolls. My stomach growled.

"Have you been here all night?" I asked Mateo, crossing two fingers behind my back in hopes that this might work.

"Uh . . . yeah."

"Without a break?"

He nodded. "So?"

"So . . . I bet you're getting hungry."

"I'm twenty-two. I'm always hungry."

Score. I smiled. "How would you like to make a deal?"

———

"WHAT THE HELL ARE YOU DOING?"

My eyes whipped up from the floury mess on the prep table as an angry man stormed into the kitchen.

Angry, but handsome. Mateo handsome. This had to be another Eden.

I scrunched up my nose, doing my best to look apologetic. I mean, I wasn't sorry, but I faked it anyway. "Making scones."

"Scones." He crossed his arms over his wide chest and his eyes flared. "Why?"

The door behind him burst open and Mateo rushed inside. "Sorry. Shit."

"What's going on, Matty?" the other man asked.

"Knox, this is Cleo. She's a pastry chef in LA. She was hungry and Lyla wasn't open yet, so we, uh . . . she made cinnamon rolls. They're freaking amazing. Better than Mom's."

"Thanks, Mateo." My chest swelled with pride. And I was right—brothers.

"What the hell? You let a stranger use my kitchen." Knox huffed. "And I'm telling Mom you said that."

"She's not a stranger," Mateo said. "She's a guest."

"Guests don't come into the kitchen." Knox turned his attention to me and hooked a thumb over his shoulder. "It's six thirty now and Lyla's got her shop open. Not to be rude but get out."

"Right." I held up a flour-covered finger. "About that. I, uh . . . can't."

There was no way I was leaving this kitchen. I was finally feeling like myself thanks to the baking, cinnamon roll and two additional cups of coffee I'd sipped while working. Besides, the only thing waiting for me outside this room was a grouchy bodyguard who planned to drag my ass to California today.

"Why?" Knox arched an eyebrow. His chiseled jaw was dusted with stubble and his fit physique showed through even his boxy chef's coat. Too bad I hadn't met someone like him in culinary school. I might have won him over with my dark chocolate cupcakes and peanut butter frosting.

Knox seemed like the kind of guy who would appreciate my bestselling cupcakes, unlike Austin. No matter what flavor I gave him, Austin greeted my cupcakes with a grimace. Even the day I'd made him a special variety pack, twelve different types nestled in my signature periwinkle box. I'd handed him the gift, and he'd sneered, then informed me that his team would love them.

Not him. His team.

Because heaven forbid Austin miss an opportunity to show me how much my very existence aggravated him.

Knox cleared his throat. Mateo stared at me with eyebrows raised.

"What? Oh." Knox had asked me a question. Right. "Sorry, I'm hungover. I can't leave because I'm in the middle of scones. And blueberry muffins. They're in the oven."

Knox's eyes darted to said oven, then back to the scones I'd just rolled out. "We can't serve those."

"Good." Mateo chuckled. "More for me. Can I take the extras home, Cleo?"

"Of course."

Mateo yawned, then slapped his brother's shoulder before tossing me a wink and leaving the kitchen.

"I don't suppose you have any strawberries?" I asked Knox. "I make this amazing strawberry-graham galette with lime zest and it would totally hit the spot this morning."

Knox blinked. Twice.

Austin did the same thing when I asked him questions. Strange.

"Is that a no on the strawberries? Or . . ."

That earned me another blink, but instead of the scowl that usually followed when Austin gaped at me, Knox grinned. "I'm not getting rid of you this morning, am I?"

I smiled. "Nope."

———

"WHERE THE FUCK HAVE YOU BEEN?" Austin barked. "I've been looking everywhere for you."

My shoulders fell. "You found me."

My trip to Montana was about over.

Austin ran a hand over his stubbled jaw, taking in the hotel's kitchen as he shook his head. It was rare to see him disheveled. It was a good look though, a little messy and a lot sexy.

"Have you been here all morning?" he asked.

"Yes." Baking. Hiding. Same thing.

It was ten thirty according to the clock on the wall. Had my security detail been anyone other than Austin, I might have made it until noon, but I'd figured eventually, he'd remember *predicable Cleo* was probably elbows deep in flour, yeast and sugar.

"Christ." Austin shook his head. "I was worried."

Whoops. I cringed, hating the guilt snaking down my spine. "I'm sorry. I didn't mean to make you worry. I was just hungry."

Austin waved a hand around the kitchen. "And instead of finding a morning snack at a vending machine, you decided to bake enough muffins to feed the whole fucking town."

"Not the whole town," I mumbled. "Just the guests." *And employees.*

Okay, maybe I'd gotten a bit carried away. The prep table was overloaded with cinnamon rolls and carrot cake muffins. The galette was cooling by the chocolate croissants. And I'd just taken a hot sheet pan of orange scones from the oven.

"You're probably starving." I swiped a plate from the shelf behind me and dished Austin a warm scone. He was a big guy so I added a muffin and a cinnamon roll too. Maybe the reason he never ate my food was because he wasn't hungry. But Austin had hangry written all over his gorgeous face and if there was ever a moment for him to embrace all that was my baking, this was it. "Here."

He frowned at the plate but took it from my grip, then he bit into the scone, chewed the bite for approximately a nanosecond before swallowing and setting the plate aside. "Coffee. To wash it down."

Seriously? My food didn't need to be washed down. My scones were the farthest thing from dry. *Asshole.* My temper surged. Maybe it was the champagne's lingering effects, but I swiped up the towel off the table and threw it at his head.

He caught it before it could hit him in the face. "What the hell?"

"Everyone likes my food," I snapped. "Everyone. Mateo went home already because his shift was over, but just ask Knox. People. Love. My. Food."

Why don't you?

Austin's frame stiffened. "Who are Mateo and Knox?"

On cue, the door that led from the kitchen to the dining room opened and Knox came through with an empty tray. "Blueberry muffins are gone. So is the first batch of cinnamon rolls."

"Who the hell are you?" Austin snapped.

"You're in my kitchen." Knox took the tray to the dishwasher, dropping it into the sink and not missing a beat. Then he turned and leaned against the edge, crossing his arms over his chest. "Who are you?"

The men went into a stare down and before punches could be thrown, or muffins, I jumped in to give introductions.

"Knox Eden, meet Austin Myles, chief pain in my ass and general hater of baked goods."

CHAPTER FIVE

AUSTIN

"Mind if we have a minute?" I asked Knox, doing my best to ignore the way his eyes lingered too long on Cleo's figure.

It was a gorgeous figure, curvy and fit, toned and lush —I couldn't fault the guy for good taste. But I still wanted to shove my fist into his nose. Kicking this guy's ass would only add another delay to our departure time—that was, if we could even get a flight out. We'd missed one already.

Knox nodded. "No problem."

My hands fisted at my sides and I sucked in a calming breath as he strode from the room, his smile fixed on Cleo. I was too damn tired for this. All I wanted was to get on an airplane and nap until I was in California.

Last night had been miserable. When Cleo had come out of the bathroom, fresh-faced and smelling like honey,

I'd known that sleeping beside her hadn't been an option. So I'd left to check out the hotel.

It wasn't a big building, nothing like the swank resorts I'd seen while traveling a few times with Ray. My whole inspection had taken less than an hour.

I'd done it twice.

Then I'd stepped outside, thinking I'd look around town a bit, but when the freezing cold had bitten into my skin, I'd retreated inside. I'd spent hours in the lobby, sitting in front of the fire, staring at the flames, hoping that if I waited long enough, Cleo would be asleep. When my eyelids had been too heavy to fight, I'd called it quits and returned to the room.

Cleo had been facedown in a pillow, those perfect pink lips parted enough to let a slight snore slip free. She'd barely blinked as I'd come in and made myself uncomfortable on the floor. At least the hotel had a plush carpet instead of the industrial carpets in most places.

I'd fallen asleep to Cleo's snores. I'd woken up to a kick in the gut.

I hadn't meant to fall asleep after she'd tripped over me. I'd planned to let her go search out coffee, thinking she'd bring some back for the both of us. Hours later, when I'd realized how much time had passed with me sleeping on her pillow, I'd flown into a panic.

This was why it wasn't safe for me to watch her. I let my guard down whenever I found her with flour in her chocolate hair, like there was now. She always seemed to leave a streak beside her left ear.

"I'm sorry about this morning," she said. "If it makes you feel better, Knox wasn't too happy to find me here either."

I grunted.

Unhappy? Yeah, right. That guy had been drooling over her and they sure seemed like fast friends. And she was into chefs.

Cleo had dated one last year, a guy who worked at a restaurant a few blocks down from Crumbs. Their relationship had been brief but painful. Every day, I'd get a report from whoever was assigned her detail on exactly what she and Chef John had done. Dinner. Movie. Make-out session in his car.

Those had been an agonizing three weeks and six days.

Cleo gave me a small smile. "Merry Christmas Eve."

"Merry Christmas Eve."

"Are you sure you're not hungry?"

I nodded. "I'm good."

"Here." She put one of the muffins on a plate and held it out. "Try this."

"It's okay." I held up a hand. "I'm not hungry." Worrying about her had put a knot in my stomach that had yet to shake loose.

"Just try it." She walked around the table, bringing me the plate.

"I don't want a muffin."

"But if you try it, you might like it."

"I don't want it, Cleo."

"But if you try it—"

"I don't want a goddamn muffin," I snapped, instantly regretting it when her face fell. "Fuck. I'm sorry."

She tossed the plate aside, the ceramic bouncing and the muffin rolling off the plate, dropping over the edge of the table to the floor. "Fine."

Her fingers flew to the ties on her apron, ripping and tugging until it was free. Then she yanked it over her head, balled it up and threw it.

At my face.

The white cloth and a cloud of flour smacked me in the nose before I could block it. When I set the apron aside, Cleo was marching for the door.

"Damn it." I shook my head, giving her a head start before chasing out of the kitchen after her. I caught her in the lobby on the way to the elevator. "Look, I'm sorr—"

My phone rang. I tugged it out of my pocket, Ray's name flashing on the screen. *Shit.*

"Cleo, wait."

She didn't listen. She pushed the up arrow and the second the doors slid open, she disappeared inside.

I wasn't sure which Hillcrest to deal with first. I decided on the less terrifying of the two and answered my phone. "Ray."

"Austin, I understand you sent the pilot home with the plane yesterday. An empty plane."

"Yes, I sent him home. Cleo didn't want to leave so I agreed to stay one night."

"Together?"

"Yes, sir." There was no point in avoiding details. "The hotel was sold out. I slept on the floor."

His silence was reaction enough.

"We'll be leaving for the airport soon," I said.

"She's not answering my calls. Tell her I expect her to come straight here when you arrive."

Ray didn't wait for my confirmation before ending the call. He didn't need agreement. He'd issued an order and I would see it through.

One more year. I had to make it through one more year of working with Ray, then I'd take a pay cut from my own salary and cut him loose. But I had to make it another year. Two would be ideal, but one minimum.

Channing was two years away from graduating college and I refused to let my brother go into debt while he earned his degree. I also refused to let my mother go into debt paying for his education.

Mom had sacrificed enough for us both. All I wanted was for her to sail into retirement and enjoy an easier pace of life.

She'd worked tirelessly my entire life to provide for me and Channing. Christmas hadn't ever been the lavish affair it was for the Hillcrests, but Mom had spoiled us in her own way, with one big gift that she saved for and chose with care. On our birthdays, she'd bake us a special cake.

I'd never cared that my jeans were secondhand and my shoes weren't name brand. For a long time, it had been Mom and me, the Myles team.

Dad had died in a work accident when I'd been three, and though they'd had some money stashed away, she'd used it to pay off our house so we'd never have to move. She'd given me that stability. Then when I'd been in middle school, she'd introduced me to the mailman who'd become more than a mailman.

Eddy had been a good man. A good father and stepfather. A good husband.

He'd died before Channing's second birthday. Cancer.

I was thirteen years older than Channing and after Eddy passed, I'd done all I could to help Mom raise him. She hadn't needed my help—as far as humans went, my mother was the strongest on earth. But I'd helped regardless. She'd endured enough.

Mom and I had both insisted that Channing get a college degree. He had the brains for it and I made a decent profit each year to pay for it.

But I needed Ray.

Even though I wanted Cleo.

I walked to the elevator and pushed the button, unsure of what I'd find when I made it to the fourth floor. Hopefully Cleo standing beside a packed suitcase. Instead, I stepped into the room and was hit with a cloud of honeyed steam billowing from the bottom of the bathroom door. The shower was running.

This woman truly hated me.

How was I supposed to sit in here when she was naked twenty feet away? I spun for the door, escaping the room and that luscious smell. No matter how cold it was outside, I had to get the hell out of this building.

The elevator would be too slow, so I found the staircase, jogged to the first floor and took the nearest door marked exit.

The cold air was a son of a bitch, biting into my flesh, but I gritted my teeth, cursing this miserable state with every step toward the coffee shop. When I walked inside, the patrons all stared. Probably because I was the idiot Californian in Montana without a damn coat.

I stomped to the counter, dug out my wallet and slapped it on the counter. "Black coffee. Hot as you can make it. Then a muffin and a scone. Please."

The barista nodded and left me to prepare my order.

With my food and drink in hand, I found an empty table as far away from the door as I could get. I inhaled the muffin before taking a bite. It was good, not incredible, but I was starving. Cleo had been right about that.

Buying other people's baked goods had become this sick game. Nothing was ever as good as the food Cleo tried to force-feed me, the food I pretended was marginal at best. Instead of marveling at the culinary creations made by a woman I couldn't have, I ate from other bakers.

Because there were other bakers in the world. Just like there were other women.

I inhaled the muffin and scone, scalding my tongue on the coffee, then checked my watch. Cleo normally took an hour to get ready for the day.

I'd spent enough mornings in my car before dawn, watching her lights turn on around the house before she pulled out of her garage almost exactly sixty minutes later and drove to work. Now that she knew about her security detail, there was no point in keeping up the act. It would be smart for her to vary the routine once in a while too.

My team was trained and damn good at blending into the shadows, but so were criminals. If something happened to her . . .

I shoved that thought away and chugged a burning gulp of coffee. Nothing was going to happen to Cleo. She would be fine. Even when I quit working for Ray, he'd find someone equally as capable to keep her safe.

Besides, this morning was a good example of how my game slipped when she was around.

After twenty minutes of waiting, Cleo had had enough time to get out of the shower and put some clothes on, so I took my muffin wrapper to the trash, nodded a silent thanks to the barista and set out into the Arctic.

My teeth chattered as I made my way to the hotel. My goose bumps had goose bumps. Why hadn't I brought a damn coat? Right. Because the plan had been to get in and get out.

The hotel lobby was quiet as I walked for the staircase, hoping four flights would warm me up. When I reached the room and slid my key card into the door, Cleo's scent hit me once more and sent a rush of blood to my groin.

I was tempted to plug my nose. Instead, I opted to breathe through my mouth.

The door to the bathroom flew open and Cleo emerged, her hair wet and twisted in a knot. Her face was bare and flushed from the shower, but at least she was dressed. Her designer distressed jeans fit like a second skin and her black tank top left none of her curves to my imagination.

Fuck, she looked beautiful. Stunning, really. There wasn't a Hollywood starlet who could rival Cleo's beauty. My heart skipped and my throat went dry.

I dropped my eyes to the floor. "We missed the morning flight, but there's another at three."

We'd get to California late, but at least we'd be home and we could go our separate ways. This was the most time I'd spent with Cleo lately and it was too much. She was too perfect. Too irresistible. I didn't trust myself not to lose the stern and rude disguise.

And without those acting as a barrier to my true emotions, she would see right through me.

That was not a conversation I wanted to have on Christmas.

"Do you need help with your suitcase?" I asked.

"Oh, I'm not going."

"What?" My face whipped up as she disappeared into the bathroom. I followed. "Say that again."

"I'm not going," she told me through the mirror as she untied her hair and picked up a paddle brush, dragging it carefully through her long locks. "I booked this vacation. I'm taking it."

"Goddamn, you are difficult."

"Difficult?" Her brushstrokes moved faster. "How am I difficult? I don't want to leave. I don't have to leave."

"Yes, you do."

"I'll call my father and explain. If you're worried about your job, don't be."

"If I don't bring you home, you and I both know Ray will fire me before the new year."

"No, he won't. I'll make sure he understands this was my decision and that if he fires you, I'll never speak to him again."

I believed her.

She'd fight for my job. She'd go head-to-head against her father.

Even though she hated me.

Because Cleo Hillcrest was the finest person I'd ever met. It would be unfair of Ray to fire me, and she knew it. She fought for what was right. Cleo had a pure heart and a kind soul. She put others before herself, which was why this jaunt to Montana was so strange. She might hate the Hillcrest Christmas fiasco, but for years I'd watched her endure it because her father had asked her to.

I didn't blame her for needing an escape, but I wouldn't risk her safety for it.

"I can't leave you here," I said. I couldn't leave her, period.

Maybe the real reason I didn't want to cleave my relationship with Ray was because that meant I'd lose my connection to Cleo. Even on the days when she was assigned to someone else, I had that tether. Cutting it was probably for the best. My sanity was on the brink as it was. But I couldn't leave her.

Cleo set her brush down, turning to me with a sigh. "I'm going to relax and enjoy this room. I'm going to wander around town and eat too much. Then I'll come home after Christmas and get back to work. I'm fine alone."

She stepped closer and the room shrank. My heart raced as she looked up at me with those bright hazel eyes and in that moment, I would have promised her the world for just one kiss of those soft lips.

"Go home, Austin. Please. Go home."

The plea in her voice did me in. This was one of the few times I'd witnessed Cleo say to hell with what everyone else wanted and go her own way. She wanted this vacation and I wouldn't be the man who stole it from her.

"Okay."

"Okay?"

I nodded. "Okay."

A smile tugged at her mouth. "Thank you."

I swallowed hard, unable to tear my eyes away. Her lips were soft and pink. The bottom was fuller than the top, but not by much. Just enough for a sexy, natural pout. What would happen if I kissed her? What would happen if I gave in to the temptation?

Cleo would knee me in the balls.

I'd lose my contract with Ray, and he'd destroy my reputation.

My employees would be jobless and I'd ruin my company.

Kissing her . . . it would be almost worth it.

"Austin," she whispered, forcing my eyes to hers.

Cleo's head cocked to the side. Her eyebrows came together.

And I took a step away.

"I'll let your father know we're staying."

She nodded as I took another step back, but before I could leave the bathroom, her hand shot out and wrapped around my elbow. "Wait. What do you mean 'we'?"

CHAPTER SIX

CLEO

"What about this one?"

"I don't care," Austin muttered.

I frowned and went to the next style on the rack of men's coats. "This one?"

"I don't care."

That was the sixth *I don't care* since we'd arrived at Quincy Farm and Feed. "You have to buy a coat."

"Why?" He crossed his arms over his chest.

"Your lips are blue." My eyes dropped to his mouth. The purple tinge wasn't as attractive as their normal pink color, but I wanted to kiss them regardless. Just once. Since that wasn't going to happen, I focused on the task at hand and took a hunter-green coat off its hanger. "Here."

He took it from my hands and draped it over his arm.

"Put it on." It was an extra-large so I was sure it would fit.

"Don't you think we should buy it first? Unless you have more *shopping* to do."

"No." This was a nice enough store, but I wasn't in the market for farm supplies and bulk pet food. The only reason we'd come here was because we'd learned at the hotel that this was the only store in town open on Christmas Eve that carried men's coats.

Austin had argued that if we stayed indoors, the coat was unnecessary. Maybe he was fine sitting on the bed, working on his laptop while I watched TV, but I was most definitely not. Close proximity to Austin was not an option.

Either he'd do something to piss me off and I'd be forced to smother that handsome face in a down pillow. Or he'd give me one of those rare gifts, a small smile or a gentle look, like the one he'd given me in the bathroom when he'd relented to this vacation.

Those precious moments, though very few and very far between, were like pouring gasoline on my crush's fire.

I lived for those moments. If the two of us were trapped in a hotel room, I might forget myself and do something epically humiliating and stupid. Like lick the stubble on his face as if it were cream cheese frosting.

Yummy.

Smothering and licking were not options, so instead, I'd dragged Austin out of the hotel. My agenda for the holiday had been completely upended. Though I did like to wander.

"Okay, let's go." I led the way to the checkout counter. "I'll pay for it."

Austin scowled and stepped close, forcing me away from the credit card reader with that beefy physique. He dug his wallet from his jeans, bought the coat and ripped the tags free, shrugging it on before walking to the door.

"Anywhere you want to go?" I asked, looking up and down the sidewalk.

"California."

"No one's stopping you," I singsonged with a saccharine smile. Before we'd ventured out of the room, I'd spent a solid twenty minutes attempting to convince him to go home without me. The stubborn ass had refused.

Austin gave me a look that said he wasn't having that debate again.

"Fine," I muttered. "If you're going to stay here with me, is there anything you'd like to see?"

"No."

"Are you sure?"

Austin stared at me, his mouth clamped shut. He did this a lot. I'd repeat a question, double-checking because double-checking was polite, thank you very much. But he'd just stand there, silently reminding me that he'd already given his answer and it wasn't going to change.

I threw my hands in the air and spun around. "Then I'll decide."

Austin fell in step beside me, still quiet. He stayed on his side of the sidewalk, far enough away that there was no risk of touching but close enough he could shove me out of the way if I was in danger.

The stubble on his jaw caught the morning sunlight. The air was dry and cold, giving his cheeks a pink flush. It was a bright and cheerful day, despite the freezing temperature. Fresh snow glittered under the cloudless blue sky, turning Quincy into a winter wonderland.

I took in a long breath, blowing it out in a white stream of frozen air. A bell dinged as a woman stepped out of a shop ahead. I slowed and looked inside the front window decked out in Christmas bows and greenery. The scent of apples wafted from the door, mixing with the fresh mountain air.

I veered to the door, knowing Austin would follow. It was a kitchen shop, its back wall lined with a row of glass containers filled with flavored oils and vinegars.

"Good morning," the clerk greeted, removing a pair of spectacles perched on her nose. "Happy Holidays."

"Happy Holidays." I smiled, my eyes wide as I took it all in. This was certainly not the kind of store I'd expected to see in such a small town. Hand-carved cutting boards made an artful spread on a round table in the center of the small space. Along one wall, an array of hooks held different utensils and kitchen embellishments.

I walked to a cutting board, my fingers running across the smooth wood grain. "This is beautiful."

"Thank you." The woman came around the cashier's counter. "Would you like some apple cider?"

"Please." I nodded, taking the cup from her when she brought it over. Austin—typical—shook his head and declined. I sipped the hot drink, the flavor bursting on my tongue. "This is delicious."

"My own recipe." She smiled, tucking a lock of gray hair behind her ear. "Shopping for anything in particular today?"

"Just browsing. We're from out of town and exploring today."

"There are quite a few of us open," she said. "Mostly for the, er, gentlemen around town doing some last-minute gift buying."

As if she'd conjured one from thin air, the bell on the door dinged and a man came inside with a wave. "Morning, Sandy. I'm in a bit of a rush. I, uh—"

"Haven't bought anything for your wife yet," she finished. "Or your mother."

The man shrugged with a sheepish grin and Sandy went about pulling items from tables, getting his okay with each before ringing him up and fancying up two different gift bags.

I lingered, sipping my cider and choosing three spatulas and one board to take home.

Austin was standing stoically beside the door, his shoulders pinned, when his phone rang. He dug it from his pocket and looked at the screen, his frame relaxing at whatever he saw. I expected him to go outside, but he just put the phone to his ear. "Hi, Mom."

I tried not to eavesdrop on his quiet conversation as I perused, but it was hard not to catch his every word in a store this size.

"Merry Christmas Eve," he said. "I know. I'm sorry I'll miss it too."

He was missing Christmas with his family because of me. My heart sank. Damn it. I'd been so worried about myself, I hadn't thought of what this would do to him. Maybe I was as selfish as he'd proclaimed.

"Okay, Mom. Enjoy. I'll give you a call when I get home." He paused. "Yeah. Dinner sounds great. Love you."

I'd stopped shopping when he ended the call and slid his phone into his pocket. I was staring.

Austin's gaze came to mine, holding it for just a moment before looking away. The cheese grater seemed to pull his focus.

I sighed and went to the register, letting Sandy package my things now that the other man had his gifts and was headed out the door. When she had everything bagged, I thanked her again for the cider.

Austin appeared at my side with a cutting board in his hand.

"That's nice," I said.

"Yeah." He took out his credit card and paid before I waved goodbye and led the way outside.

"Mind if we walk some more?" I asked, already knowing his answer. But I asked anyway. Because despite what he thought of me, I was considerate of his feelings. At least, normally.

"Fine by me." He shortened his strides and let me set the pace.

"Who did you buy the cutting board for?" I asked as we walked down the block.

"My mom."

"Why don't you go home? Give it to her tomorrow."

"She works tomorrow. We celebrate Christmas Eve together."

"Austin." I stopped, shaking my head. "Go home. Please. Be with your family."

"By the time I get there tonight, she'll be asleep. She works early."

"Oh."

He waited for me to continue walking. He always did that. I wasn't sure if that was part of the bodyguard handbook or if he was simply being respectful, but I liked that he always had my back.

"What does your mom do?" I asked but didn't expect an answer. Austin rarely spoke of himself or his personal life.

"She's a nurse. She likes to work on holidays because they pay her time and a half. And since my brother and I are grown, we don't care if we celebrate on Christmas Eve or Christmas Day or whenever."

"Ah." I nodded. "And your father?"

"He died."

"I'm sorry." *Way to be nosy, Cleo.*

"Don't be. It was a long time ago when I was young. He was a fireman and was killed in the line of duty."

"I still shouldn't pry. I'm—"

"It's okay, Cleo."

Cleo. How I loved my name in his voice when he wasn't angry with me. It was like a deep, resonating note. Musical and sultry.

We passed another open shop and the window display lured me inside. It was a jewelry store that specialized in silver. I found a beautiful cuff with an oval turquoise stone in the center. I bought it for Brynne, then a pair of silver earrings for myself. All the while, Austin stood by the exit, waiting for me to finish.

Traffic on Main Street had picked up by the time we made it to the edge of downtown. The sun had warmed the road and as vehicles passed, their tires slushed through the snow.

"I like Quincy," I said as we crossed the street, strolling toward the hotel. "It's charming."

"Their airport leaves a lot to be desired," Austin grumbled.

I laughed. "It is very tiny."

My flight here had required three stops. One from California to Salt Lake, then Salt Lake to Missoula. The last leg to Quincy had been on a propeller plane and I'd gripped my armrest the entire time. Thirty minutes had felt like three hours.

I waved a hand toward The Eloise. "I like that the tallest building downtown is the hotel."

It stood proud as the focal point on the street, yet it was a pebble compared to the snow-covered mountains in the distance. On the wall that faced our way, a large wreath decorated the brick façade.

Garlands draped over Main Street, glittering in the bright light. Each of the stores we'd passed had a festive window display. Even the offices that were closed seemed full of the holiday spirit.

"This is how Christmas is supposed to be," I said. "Festive but peaceful."

"Agreed." Austin nodded.

"That might be the first thing we've ever agreed on. And this is definitely the longest conversation we've ever had."

"No, it's not."

"Yes, it is."

"What about all the days I was at the bakery getting the security up to snuff?"

"Talking about cameras and exit protocol is not a conversation." I held up a hand before he could argue. "It's okay. I know you don't like me. I just hope that we can get along while we're here."

"It's not that I don't like you, Cleo."

"Sure it is." I shrugged, pretending like the truth didn't hurt. "But I appreciate your dedication to my father and our family. Especially when that means you have to put up with me."

"That's not—" Austin raked a hand through his hair and hesitated. Maybe he wanted to lie, to tell me that I wasn't a huge pain in his ass. But we both knew it would be a lie, so in predictable Austin form, he simply stayed quiet.

"I think I'm going to head inside." I pointed to the hotel. Despite my coat and the sunshine, the warmth from my cider had worn off and the cold had seeped into my bones.

"I'm going to head to the gas station down the block. Buy a few toiletries. Are you going to be in the room?"

"Actually, I'm going to hang out in the lobby. Maybe read on my phone by the fire."

"Please don't run off. Text me if you change plans."

"I will," I promised.

"Then I'll see you in a bit." With a nod, he turned and strode down the street.

Austin's long legs ate up the sidewalk, and with his hands in his coat pockets, his shoulders looked broader than ever.

Don't look at his ass. I looked. How was I supposed to resist a quick peek? Ogling Austin's perfectly sculpted behind was my Christmas Eve present to myself.

Luckily, he didn't notice. He was too busy putting half the town of Quincy between us.

Ugh. This stupid crush. The sad part was, no matter

how much he insulted me or how many times I was forced to throw something at his head, I didn't want the crush to end. I hadn't met a man worth taking Austin's place in my fantasies. Even if he was sometimes a jerk and always a grouch, he was still the dream.

With a sigh, I trudged inside. The hotel lobby was warm and inviting, but with every step, I felt more and more like I was in the wrong place. The right thing to do for Austin would be to pack my things and get him home for Christmas Eve.

I walked to one of the couches, plopping down in front of the fireplace, and took the phone from my purse to search for flights. There was one. The last flight from Quincy to Los Angeles was scheduled to leave in ten minutes. We'd never make it.

But what if we drove to a bigger town? I checked flight options from Missoula. The last left at eight this evening. It was a two-hour drive and the flight would get us home after midnight, but he'd be home for Christmas Day. If we left within the next hour, we could make it.

I surged off the couch and gathered my things, jogging toward the elevator. It took forever for the car to return to the lobby. *Hurry up. Hurry up.* Finally, it chimed and I stepped inside, hitting the button for floor four. The doors had never closed slower. The ride up was agonizing.

Squeezing through the doors, I raced for the room, fumbling with the key card to get inside. Then I dropped my purse and shopping haul, tearing off my coat as I sprinted for the closet and my empty suitcase. The drawers were empty in a flash. My toiletries were thrown into their travel bag. I was sitting on the case, sandwiching it closed to get the zipper shut, when the room door opened and Austin stepped inside, carrying a plastic sack.

"What are you doing?" he asked.

"Packing. If we leave now and drive to Missoula, we can get on the last flight—"

"Cleo, no."

"What do you mean, no? We need to hurry." I snapped my fingers and pointed to my suitcase. "Would you help me zip this, please?"

Austin shook his head. "I've already booked my flight for the day after Christmas to match yours. We're staying."

"But—"

"We're staying. It's too late."

"It's not too late." My shoulders fell. "I don't want you to have to stay here and spend Christmas with someone you don't even like."

He tossed his plastic sack aside and crossed the room. "I like you."

Oh, how I wished that were true. "It's okay. You don't have to pretend."

"I like you, Cleo." He stepped even closer, his hands coming to my shoulders.

My heart stopped. Actually stopped. Austin didn't touch me. Ever. Unless it was by mistake. But the weight of his wide hands and the warmth of his palms seeped through my sweater and into my skin.

"We'll stay."

I barely registered his words. He smelled so good, like spicy cologne and fresh air and a scent that was wholly Austin. Why did he have to smell so good? I resisted the urge to drop my nose into his chest and take a long pull. "Are you sure?"

There I was, double-checking again.

Austin didn't answer.

Except instead of annoyance on his face, he wore a different expression, one I couldn't make sense of. His forehead was furrowed, almost like he was in pain. His lips were pursed in a thin line. But his eyes. They told a completely different story. They were intense and dark, the brown a deeper shade than normal and utterly mesmerizing.

Maybe he didn't like me.

Or maybe . . .

Before I could indulge in the fantasy that he might like me, just a little, Austin tore his hands away from my shoulders, turned to swipe up the plastic bag from the floor and strode into the bathroom, closing the door behind him and flipping the lock.

Two seconds later, the sound of the shower's spray drifted into the room.

I flopped off my suitcase and onto the bed, groaning to the ceiling.

Why couldn't we be friends? Life would be easier if we were friends. Why couldn't I get rid of this stupid crush?

"I want to go home," I grumbled. Montana had been a huge mistake.

But I was here. Austin was resigned to the idea of staying and as every minute passed, our chances of getting home to LA by Christmas dwindled.

It was time to make the best of an awkward situation. I shoved myself up off the bed and quickly unpacked my suitcase. Then as the shower turned off, I scribbled a note to Austin that I'd gone to the lobby. He was naked on the other side of the bathroom door. There was no way I'd be able to hide the blush in my cheeks when he came out.

So I slipped from the room and went to the lobby. There was a new clerk at the desk when I approached. "Hello. I was just wondering if I could reserve a place in the dining room for dinner tonight."

"Of course." The clerk smiled and took down my reservation.

"Thanks."

If Christmas Eve was Austin's time to celebrate, then I'd do my best to make this trip enjoyable. Starting with dinner.

CHAPTER SEVEN

AUSTIN

"Hey," I answered Channing's call. "How's it going?"

"Good. Just wanted to call and make sure you haven't frozen your balls off yet."

I chuckled. "Not quite. Sorry I'm not there today."

Instead, I was back at the farm supply store with two long-sleeved thermals draped over one arm while I stared at the packages of boxer briefs and crew socks. I'd taken a shower but wearing yesterday's clothes was getting old. I could survive in the same jeans for the rest of the trip, but I wasn't going to wear the same damn underwear.

I probably should have stopped at the store after my trip to the gas station for toiletries, but at this point, I didn't mind making multiple trips. There wasn't much else to do today.

"I'll make it up to you at New Year's," I told Channing.

"It's cool," he said. "Mom and I are good. She's cooking all my favorite stuff today because she feels guilty for not being home on Christmas."

That was how Mom was every year. She'd spend all of Christmas Eve in the kitchen, making more food than Channing and I could eat all week, let alone in one day, just so that on Christmas Day we weren't fending for ourselves.

Then she'd come home from her shift at the hospital and we'd eat leftovers. Mom didn't make the traditional Christmas roast or ham or turkey. She went straight to our favorites: homemade lasagna and green chili enchiladas. They reheated well in the microwave too.

"I wish I was there," I said.

"Gotta deal with the diva."

"She's not a diva." I frowned, grabbing a four-pack of boxers and a bundle of black socks.

"Dude, any chicks that you have to protect are total divas."

"Not Cleo."

"Then why'd she take off to Montana for some bougie vacation?"

"She just came to be alone."

"Diva."

"Would you stop calling her a diva?" I snapped. "She isn't like that."

"Whoa. Sorry," he muttered.

"No, it's not you." I sighed. "I'm on edge."

Being on this trip, being this close to Cleo, was making me an exceptionally grumpy bastard.

There was a clicking in the background, like Channing was pressing buttons. My guess was that while Mom was in the kitchen, he was playing video games. I'd never really been into the things myself, but on holidays like this, I'd make an exception and let him school me at a game.

"Wish I was there," I repeated. Though it was only partially the truth. Cleo was magnetic and enchanting. Time with her was never a waste, no matter how painful it was to maintain my restraints.

"Yeah," Channing said. "At least you don't have to go to some rich-dude party."

"True." The Hillcrests threw an outlandish Christmas Eve celebration and Ray liked to have security inside and outside the house. My team would be there tonight, like they were every year. My second-in-command, Blake, would be there himself and no matter what came up, he'd handle it.

When I'd first started Garrison, I'd both managed the business and taken on client tasks. But as we'd grown, I'd cut my time with clients. I focused on risk assessments and pairing team members with jobs. I built relationships with my customers and trained my team, most of whom were ex-military, to our protocols.

I trusted each and every one of them while they were

in the field, so attending events and parties personally hadn't been something I'd done for years.

Especially when it came to the Hillcrests. It was too much to see Cleo decked out in a shimmering gown, the fabric skimming over her curves, and her smile bright— fake, but beautiful nonetheless.

I passed a rack of sweatpants and swiped up a pair in light gray. They'd be better to sleep in tonight than my jeans when I camped out on the floor.

"Anything else happening?" I asked Channing.

"Nah." His attention had clearly turned back to his game, not that he was all that talkative on the phone anyway. Getting any idea how his classes were going was like pulling teeth.

The two of us did better in person. I'd find some time next week to take him out for lunch or dinner and make sure he was good. "Okay, I'll let you go. Give Mom a hug for me. And don't eat everything. I'll be back the day after Christmas and there better be enchiladas."

He laughed. "No promises."

I ended the call and took another look around the store for anything else I needed. There wasn't. Everything I'd bought would fit in my backpack. Tonight, I'd work on my laptop, answering emails and reading reports. Hopefully that would be enough of a distraction from Cleo in the bed wearing those skimpy pajamas. Though it would be harder to mask my attraction in sweats.

"Back again?" the clerk asked as I approached the

register and set my things down. "I thought you'd come back to get a last-minute gift for your girlfriend. That's pretty much what everyone shopping is doing today."

"She's not, uh . . . no. This is just for me."

Damn it. Should I buy Cleo a gift? I hadn't even thought about that. Why would I? If I got her something, that would make it weird, right? But it was Christmas.

Maybe I could grab her something from that kitchen store. Cleo had more kitchen utensils than any person on earth but she'd been eyeing some sort of spatula. Would she see through the gift? Would she know that I'd been watching her every move in that store, not because I was concerned with her safety, but because I could barely keep my eyes off her?

Fuck my life. When had a spatula become so complicated?

"Cash or card?" While I'd been debating the merits of a goddamn spatula, the clerk had rung up my purchases and bagged them to go.

"Oh, sorry." I dug out my wallet and swiped my card through the machine. Then I took my things and left. I forced myself across the street so I wouldn't be tempted to go inside the kitchen goods shop.

If Cleo were mine, I'd buy her all the kitchen trinkets her drawers could hold. I'd get her tasteful gifts, ones that she'd appreciate, as opposed to the too-fancy jewels her father bought her every Christmas that she never wore.

She'd appreciate a pair of simple earrings and a new

rolling pin better than the Tesla he'd bought her last year. The Tesla that she'd sold two weeks later, donating the proceeds to charity.

Blake had been with her that day. He'd laughed and rolled his eyes at Ray, then he'd praised Cleo for being the breath of fresh air that she was.

She didn't need a new car. What she needed was a weekend in Montana to unwind.

That could be my gift to her. These couple of days.

When I got back to the hotel, I walked through the doors and looked toward the fireplace. Cleo was on one of the couches, her eyes glued to her phone. She'd been in the same place when I'd left earlier.

I crossed the lobby, standing beside her couch. "Hey."

"Hey." A natural smile spread across her face as she looked up. She smiled at everyone and it was always genuine. Those smiles, combined with her baked goods, were the reason people flocked to her bakery. Cleo was magnetic. "Where'd you go?"

I held up the bag. "Bought a couple things so I could change."

"Oh." Her shoulders fell. "Sorry."

"Stop apologizing. I'm going to head on up and change, then do some work. I'll be out of your hair so you can chill in the room."

"Actually, I made us a dinner reservation."

"Oh." I grimaced. An intimate Christmas Eve dinner with this beautiful woman would be torture.

Cleo's smile disappeared. "I can cancel."

"No, don't." If dinner was what she wanted, then I'd eat with her.

For so long, I'd pretended to be a professional. I'd maintained a *professional* distance. I'd kept our interactions *professional*. I'd stayed away from her to maintain *professionalism*.

If professional actually meant acting like a rude, motherfucking asshole, I had professional nailed.

Cleo hadn't deserved my attitude. For the last day, for the last four years, I'd been acting like an ass. Keeping up the act was exhausting.

Today, I would attempt being a *true* professional.

"Dinner sounds great. Thank you." I gestured to my shirt. "But I don't have anything nice to wear."

"Neither do I. And I checked with the dining room. It's not fancy. We can come as we are."

"Okay, then. What time?"

Her face lit up into a beaming smile. "Seven thirty."

That gave me four hours to get my shit together, stop pouting and quit ruining her vacation. "I'll be there."

———

"THIS IS SO GOOD." Cleo closed her eyes and hummed. The look of rapture on her face was more mouthwatering than the chocolate cake on my fork. She opened her eyes and smiled. "How's yours?"

I dropped my gaze to my plate and cleared my throat. "Good."

"Want to try some cheesecake?"

"No, thanks." I shoved a bite in my mouth and looked anywhere but at her.

We were the only two left in the dining room. There'd been two large parties here tonight, but both had disbanded and left an hour ago.

Cleo and I had eaten at a leisurely pace. There hadn't been much conversation, but thanks to the others in the room, we'd spent the time people watching. The other guests had graciously let us stare while they'd eaten, laughed and opened gifts. Cleo and I had both ordered steaks. Not an ounce had been left behind on either of our plates. They'd been that good.

"More?" Cleo lifted the bottle of red wine between us.

"Sure." I held the stem of my glass as she poured.

"I like this version of Austin."

"The one who drinks?"

She giggled, topping off her own glass. "Yes. He's chill."

"You're the first person to ever call me chill." I took another bite of my cake followed by a sip of wine, and the last shred of tension over this meal melted away.

I let myself *chill* and enjoy her company.

"Did you always want to own a bakery?" I asked.

"Yes. My mom used to let me help her in the kitchen.

She'd let me mash bananas for banana bread and she'd measure out ingredients so I could dump them in the mixing bowl. I was so little when she died, but I never forgot those days in the kitchen. When I got older, it was something I could do to feel connected to her."

There was nothing but adoration and love in her eyes whenever she spoke of her mother. It wasn't often, but enough to see that Cleo carried Janet in her heart. Maybe that was why her food was out of this world. It was infused with love.

"What about you?" she asked. "Did you always want to be in private security?"

"I don't know if anyone in this business plans on being in this business." At least, that was how it was for all of my guys. "I just fell into it. I always wanted to be a fireman, like my dad. My mom wanted me to get my degree first, but I'd planned on applying to a station as soon as I had one. Then a month before graduation, I met this guy who owned a security firm. He was looking for some muscle to work at a few events."

Most of the other twenty-something-year-old guys he'd hired had been bored as hell. They'd hated standing against the wall, observing a party instead of participating in it. But I'd liked the work. It was interesting to watch people when they didn't realize they were being watched.

I'd seen men check out women other than their dates. I'd heard women talk about other women. And I'd learned how it felt when the tension in a crowd spiked before a fight broke out.

"I was working this concert. It was a private deal in a hotel for a twenty-first birthday party. The birthday boy was a spoiled rich kid. His dad was an actor—and no, I can't tell you who."

"Bummer." She pouted.

"I'd just turned twenty-two and was weeks away from graduating. My class load was light so whatever jobs he gave me, I took because I wanted the cash. So I'm at this concert and these two hothead assholes are about to get in a fight over a girl. I broke it up without breaking any bones or making a scene. No big deal, but my boss was there that night. He watched the whole thing. Before we left that night, he offered to train me and give me a job that paid three times what I would have made in one year as a firefighter. I couldn't pass it up."

"How long did you work for him?" Cleo asked.

"About five years. He retired, moved to Hawaii, and I decided to start Garrison." I'd built my company slowly and deliberately, only hiring crew members when I could guarantee their income for a year. I'd been working Garrison for two years before Ray had become a client, and since, we'd grown considerably.

It was still a small company in terms of the private security firms in LA. I intended to keep it that way, choosing quality services over a massive team. Still,

Garrison was bigger than I'd ever dreamed it would be after less than a decade in business.

"Do you ever wish you had become a fireman instead?" Cleo asked.

"Occasionally," I admitted. "When I see catastrophes and those in uniform banding together, I have regrets. But mostly, I consider myself fortunate to have a good job. And I like calling the shots."

Cleo laughed. "You are rather bossy."

"Occupational hazard."

She picked up the purse she'd brought to dinner off the seat of the empty chair to her left, taking out a small wrapped box. "I got you something."

My heart dropped. *Fuck.* I should have bought her that spatula. "I, uh, didn't get you anything."

"Oh, this is nothing. I don't expect or need gifts this year. But I saw this and couldn't pass it up." She slid the box across the table.

I took it and gently unwrapped the red and gold foil paper to reveal a deck of cards. The box was a hand-painted mountain scene with the words *Welcome to Quincy* written on the face.

"I noticed you collect them."

I managed a nod. I held the box, speechless. How had she known? I collected decks of cards from all the places I'd traveled. If I had seen these myself, I would have bought them.

"I saw those in the airport yesterday when I flew in

and thought they were beautiful," she said. "If you don't like them, you won't hurt my feelings."

Wait. She'd bought them even before I'd shown up here. Why? Why would she buy me something when she hated me?

Maybe . . .

I shoved that thought aside and cleared the lump in my throat. Then I looked up, meeting her shining hazel eyes. "They're great. Thank you."

"You're welcome." She beamed. "I hope you like them."

"I do. Very much."

"Why cards?" she asked. "I think it's a cool thing to collect. Better than shot glasses or refrigerator magnets. But I always wondered why."

"My mom. She taught me to play different games when I was little, but I was rough on cards. Whenever I had money, I'd buy a new deck and beg her to teach me a new game."

"How many decks do you have?"

"No idea. But they fill up three drawers in my kitchen."

"That's a lot of cards."

And this would be my favorite deck.

Our waitress appeared beside our table, her hands clasped around a black folio that likely held our bill. "How was dessert? Can I get either of you anything else?"

"No, I think we're done," Cleo said. "Thank you. May I put this on my room?"

"Yes, of course." The woman handed her the check. "And you're welcome to take your wine if you'd like to retire to your room."

"Cleo—" I started to protest, reaching for the check, but she silenced me with a scowl. Then she signed her name on the receipt and added a tip.

"Thank you for dinner," I said after the waitress cleared our plates.

"Thank you for eating with me." Cleo stood from her chair. "Will you teach me a card game?"

"Sure."

She took her wineglass and the bottle, then led the way from the dining room. But instead of veering for the elevator, she returned to the couch in front of the fireplace where she'd been reading earlier.

"Here?"

"Or would you rather play in the room?"

"No, this is fine." I dropped to the couch and lifted the lid on my cards. The less time we spent in that bedroom, the better. "Do you know how to play gin rummy?"

"No."

I took the cards from the box and shuffled them. Then taught her to play gin. An hour later, she'd finished the bottle of wine and hadn't won a single hand. But you'd never know by the smile on her face or the twinkle in her eyes.

"Gin." I discarded my last card.

"What? Already?" She giggled and tossed her cards on the pile. "Okay, I give up. Let's play a different game. How about war? Or go fish? I might stand a chance if we play kid games."

"I learned to play gin when I was six."

"Show-off." She rolled her eyes, then lifted her hand to her mouth to cover a yawn.

"We should go up."

"No, not yet." She relaxed into the thick leather of the couch, tipping her eyes up at the stone chimney and taking in the wreath hung above the fire. "This is peaceful. I like it here."

"Me too." I collected the cards, putting them back in the box, then mirrored her position.

"Thank you, Austin." She turned her cheek to look at me. Somehow, while I'd put the cards away and she'd been sitting there, we'd gotten closer. Or maybe we'd inched closer as we'd played, using the center cushion of the couch as our card table.

Whenever it had happened, our shoulders were nearly touching. A lock of her hair had slid over the leather of the couch and brushed against the cotton of my shirt.

"For what?"

"For this break. I know it was out of character for me, but sometimes I just want to say screw it. Just do what makes my heart happy. Does that make any sense?"

"Yeah." My eyes roamed her face. Without thinking, I brought my hand up to cup her cheek.

Her breath hitched.

Tingles raced across my skin.

What the fuck was I doing?

Making my heart happy.

I leaned in closer.

And kissed Cleo.

CHAPTER EIGHT

CLEO

Someone was pounding a drum in the room next door. A really loud, extremely painful drum.

No. Wait. That was just my pulse.

"Fuck you, wine," I groaned into the pillow, squeezing my eyes shut. I hadn't even realized how much I'd had to drink last night at dinner with Austin—

I shot out of bed.

Oh. My. God.

Austin had kissed me. *Austin Myles* had kissed *me*.

He'd kissed me, right? Or had I dreamed it in my wine-hazed state?

My hand flew to my lips. They felt the same as usual. Maybe a little dry since I hadn't put on my nightly sleep balm. I traced the edges, searching for any sign that I'd kissed the handsomest, sexiest man I'd ever seen, but there was nothing.

No chafed skin. No puffy swell.

But I hadn't imagined it. I hadn't dreamed it. I clearly remembered sitting on the couch in my happy buzz when Austin dropped his lips to mine.

After that, things got fuzzy. Reality had been scraped away by the stubble on his sculpted jaw.

The kiss hadn't lasted long. There'd been no tongue or playful nips. Just Austin's soft lips on mine and the all-consuming desire for . . . more.

Oh my God. Austin had kissed me.

Why? Didn't he hate me? Wasn't I this major annoyance in his life?

And where was he?

I turned in a circle, my head spinning. The room was empty except for me. I was alone but hadn't come to the room alone. Austin had been with me. After the card game and kiss, he'd lain on the bed beside me and I'd smiled at him until I'd fallen asleep.

The pillow on his side of the bed had a noticeable dent. The quilt was rumpled because he'd slept on top of the covers while I'd burrowed in deep.

At least he hadn't suffered on the floor.

He'd slept beside me and he'd kissed me. Or had I kissed him? *Oh, shit.* My stomach turned. Did I have this entire thing turned around?

"I'm so stupid." I slapped a hand to my aching forehead.

Austin had no reason to kiss me. None. But I'd been

tipsy on wine, something that always made me flirty and forward, and I'd kissed him. Then he'd brought me upstairs and put me to bed.

The man was probably back in California by now.

I tipped my head to the ceiling and groaned. "Montana was a horrible idea."

Mortification oozed from my bones, making me cringe. I trudged to the bathroom and took in my disheveled state. My hair was everywhere and the makeup I hadn't washed off last night was smeared on my face.

At least Austin wasn't here to see the goddamn wreck I'd become. I was the farthest thing from desirable. Hell, I didn't even want to be me at the moment. So I brushed my teeth, turned on the shower and got to work collecting the shreds of my dignity.

So what if I'd kissed him? I could explain that it was a mistake and apologize. I could definitely pretend it had never happened. Once we got back to LA, I fully expected never to see Austin again, but whatever. He didn't like me anyway and maybe I'd have an easier time letting go of this crush if Austin became a distant memory.

My shower was far from relaxing with the way my hands shook. Tears pricked the corners of my eyes, but I refused to cry so I rinsed the conditioner from my hair and got out. Melodrama wasn't going to make this easier.

I dried off and wrapped a towel around my body, then dragged a brush through my hair before twisting it up in a knot. When I emerged from the bathroom, I expected to find my room empty.

But there he was. All six foot three inches of glorious man holding two white ceramic mugs. I loved The Eloise Inn, but they really needed to look into in-room coffee.

"Thought you might want this." He held out a mug.

What I wanted was to roll back time. Well, not completely. I didn't want to forget kissing Austin.

"Thank you." I took the mug as his gaze tracked down my body. My very naked body covered only with a white bath sheet.

The right thing to do would be to get dressed and talk about this far, far away from the bed that seemed to get bigger every time the two of us were in this room together. Instead, I dropped my chin and swallowed the lump in my throat.

"About last night—" I said at the same time Austin said, "I'm sorry I kissed you."

I blinked and my eyes whipped up to his. "What?"

"I'm sorry I kissed you." He didn't look sorry. There was a small smile on his mouth, and Austin never smiled at me. Never. Except he had last night, like he was right now. Those brown eyes were darker than normal. He didn't seem at all uncomfortable or upset to find me freshly showered and wearing a towel.

"*You* kissed *me*? I thought I kissed you."

"No."

"But I kissed you back."

"You did."

What the hell was happening? I was never drinking again. Clearly, some women were born capable of rational thought after two nights of drinking. Not me.

Austin stood across from me, his eyes flickering between my eyes and my mouth.

"Why?" I whispered. "Why did you kiss me?"

He turned and set his mug on the nightstand, then crossed the room. He didn't touch me but he stood close, only inches away. "You said yesterday that I didn't like you. But that's not true. I like you. I've always liked you. And I guess, I just . . . I let my guard down. I'm sorry."

My jaw dropped. "Sorry?"

"I don't want to make you uncomfortable."

"Uncomfortable?" I sounded like a parrot. A hungover parrot.

He nodded. "It was unprofessional."

"Unprofessional?"

"You're my client, Cleo."

"But you wanted to kiss me."

"Yes."

Austin had wanted to kiss me. Well, what the actual fuck did I do with this information?

My head was seconds away from exploding, like the time I'd dropped a sack of flour in the bakery and the entire thing had gone up in a white puff.

Okay, so I hadn't made a move on Austin. He'd been the one to initiate the kiss. My brain began to reengage and details from last night cleared through the wine fog. Austin had touched my face. He'd cupped my cheek. He'd been the one to lean in.

And here he was, apologizing for it. Regretting it.

"Let's forget it ever happened." I set my coffee mug on the TV stand and bent to open a drawer for some clothes. I balled up a pair of panties in my fist and hid my bra in a tee, then took out a pair of jeans.

"Cleo . . ." Austin sighed as I stood, my clothes clutched to my chest.

"It's okay."

"No, it's not."

"Please, Austin. Don't. I feel embarrassed enough as it is. I don't want you to feel guilty." I gave him a small smile, ready to run and spend Christmas Day locked in the hotel bathroom. But he stopped me with his next sentence.

"I don't feel guilty."

"Huh?" My mouth fell open. "You don't?"

"I will never feel guilty for kissing you."

I blinked. If I was confused, at least the tortured look on his face made me feel like I wasn't the only one struggling to make sense of this. "I don't understand."

"Me neither," he muttered, running a hand over his jaw. "Look, I like you."

"You said that already."

Austin stepped forward, closing the distance I'd put between us. "I know I'm not your favorite person and that I've been an asshole at times—most of the time—but I can't pretend anymore. I'm sorry for how I've treated you. Truly sorry. You didn't deserve it. I'm not proud of it."

Poof. My brain went poof.

"I like you, Cleo."

This had to be a dream because if Austin *liked me* liked me, I'd melt into a puddle. Good thing I was wearing this towel to sop it up.

"I'm sorry I kissed you." He lifted his hand and cupped my cheek, like he had last night. The zing of electricity stole the air in my lungs and I leaned into his touch.

"I'm not," I whispered.

"No?"

"No." I shook my head.

"Do you hate me?"

"Some days," I admitted.

That earned me a full-blown smile, straight white teeth and all. Puddle status was imminent.

"What is happening?"

Austin's gaze dropped to my lips. "I'm kissing you again."

"Oh," I breathed as his whisper caressed my cheek.

Then his mouth was there, hovering over mine before he dropped a kiss to the corner of my mouth. Then another. And another. He peppered my lips with kisses until I leaned in and the clothes in my arms dropped to my bare feet.

Austin's arms wrapped around me and he crushed me to his body. The gentle kisses were gone and he smashed his lips on mine. I opened, letting his tongue sweep inside. His taste exploded on my tongue and I moaned, wrapping my arms around his broad shoulders to hold him tight.

Holy fucking shit, Austin was kissing me. And my God, he was good at it. My legs trembled and I tightened my grip on his shoulders before my knees could give way.

Austin tore his mouth away and dropped his forehead to mine. "What do you want?"

"You. I've always wanted you."

He leaned back, his eyebrows coming together. "You have?"

"Come on." I giggled. "You have to know that I've had a crush on you since the day my father brought you into Crumbs."

"You had a smudge of chocolate on your cheek and your fingers were purple."

I'd been making blueberry pastries that day and the moment Austin had walked through the door, I'd chastised myself for not wearing gloves. I'd been so embarrassed that he'd seen me with purple fingers. "You were so gruff. You said five words to me."

Hi. Good to meet you.

"One look at you and I was tongue-tied. I wished I had come to the bakery before taking the job with your dad. I wished I had met you first."

I sighed, my heart squeezing. "If my father finds out, you'll lose your job."

"I will."

I unwound my arms from his neck and expected him to put me down, but his hold only got stronger and he lifted me, my toes dangling above the carpet. His eyes searched mine, waiting for me to decide.

Because that look of confidence, of complete surety, told me that Austin had already decided. He didn't care if he lost this job.

If all we had was this trip, then I didn't want to think about what happened tomorrow. I wanted to be with Austin. Just this once.

"Kiss me anyway."

He didn't have to be told twice. Austin crushed his lips to mine and the heat in the room spiked. In only a towel, I was burning up and so desperate to feel his skin against mine, I yanked and tugged at his shirt.

His tongue plundered my mouth, leaving no corner untouched. His fingertips dug into the curves of my hips as he turned us and walked us to the bed.

"Damn, Cleo, how I want you." He tore his mouth from mine and dropped it to my neck, trailing wet kisses along my skin.

"Yes." My fingers dove into his dark hair and I threaded them through the strands.

He growled against my skin, then dropped me to the edge of the bed.

I stared up as he reached behind his head and yanked off his shirt. *Oh my abs.* Was this the reason he didn't eat baked goods? Because a six-pack was a good one. I'd forgive him for every missed bite of my food if he just let me run my hands over his washboard stomach.

My mouth watered and I reached for the button of his jeans only to have my hand swatted away.

"Not yet." He dropped his gaze to the front of my towel.

I lifted a hand to undo the tuck in the terry cloth only to have my hand swatted again. "What was that for?"

"It's rude to unwrap someone else's gift."

And there it was—the puddle. It pooled between my legs.

Austin took my hand and pulled me to my feet. His finger trailed across the bare line of my shoulder, causing a shiver to race down my spine. That same finger skimmed my collarbone before dipping into the hollow of my throat. He moved slowly, taking each inch deliberately, until I was panting beneath his touch.

"Austin."

His focus was entirely on his finger as it finally reached the line of the towel. Then with a flick of his wrist, it was gone, forgotten at my feet.

I held my gaze on the hard plain of his chest, taking in the dusting of hair on his pecs. I studied the contoured muscles of his arms and how the ropes of his biceps and triceps wrapped around one another, all while he studied my body with the same intensity.

His eyes traced every curve of my breasts and the swell of my hips. They dropped to the apex of my thighs.

When I dared look up, there was so much appreciation and lust in his gaze, it stole my breath.

Austin lifted a hand to cup one of my breasts as he shuffled closer, the heat from his chest hitting mine. He rolled my nipple between his fingers, and his eyes never stopped wandering, leaving tingling trails on my skin.

"My turn." I reached between us for the waistband of his jeans. He didn't stop me as I opened the button and dragged the zipper over his straining arousal.

I ran my palm along his length, pressing hard as his erection filled my hand. He was long and thick and perfect. An ache bloomed in my core, the throb of desire matching my thundering heartbeats.

Austin hooked his finger under my chin and turned up my mouth, claiming it with his own as he laid me on the bed. Then he pulled away to strip, returning to me with a ferocity I'd never felt before.

He wanted me. I felt it in the swipe of his tongue and the firm grip of his hands. He wanted me, only me.

I'd been blind to it before, but as he kissed and sucked and licked, it all became clear. The insults. The critiques. The dismissals. He'd used them all as tools to keep me away.

With an arm around my back, Austin hoisted me deeper into the plush bed. His weight pressed me into the mattress and when I spread my legs, he relaxed into the cradle of my hips, never once breaking our kiss.

My hands roamed over the hard lines of his back, my short nails digging into the solid muscle of his body.

Every lick of his tongue and nip of his teeth made the ache in my core spike. "Austin."

He reached between us to fist his shaft but stopped. "Fuck. No condom."

"I don't care."

"Are you—"

I nodded and arched my hips. "Please."

I'd been on the pill since high school and I hadn't been with a man since college. Dating over the past four years had been nearly impossible. It was hard to date when you were infatuated with your bodyguard.

Austin dragged the tip of his cock through my folds. "God, you're wet."

"For you." Always for him.

He rocked inside, slowly, back and forth until he slid inside, filling and stretching me.

"Austin," I moaned, my throat arching up in a surge of pleasure.

"Christ, you feel good." He dropped a string of kisses down my chest until he reached the curve of my breast. Then he took a nipple in his hot mouth, biting on the hard nub, and I cried out his name again. The mix of pleasure and pain sent a rush through my veins.

Austin eased out before pumping inside again, the sound of his hips slamming into mine echoing through the room along with my whimpers.

His rhythm started slowly, deliberately, until he was moving in a motion that would definitely clue the room next door into exactly what we were doing.

Fucking. I was fucking Austin Myles. Oh, yes, I was screwing Austin and damn, but it was good. So, so good. I'd scream it from the hotel roof if they'd let me.

He was mine. For today, he was mine. And it felt so right that I closed my eyes and let the pleasure build into a blinding light. The root of his cock dragged against my clit with every thrust. He hit the spot inside that drove me wild until I was shaking, writhing beneath him.

"I'm—" I didn't get a chance to warn him. I shattered, pulsing around him as I moaned through the hardest and longest orgasm of my life.

The white spots in my vision cleared just in time to let me see the restraint on Austin's face break, and with a groan, he let go, pouring hot inside me until he collapsed onto the bed.

Our slick bodies clung to one another and I burrowed my face into his neck, savoring his scent and memorizing the weight of his body on mine.

He'd ruined me. Devastated. No one would ever compare and silly me, I hoped I wouldn't have to find out.

When we'd both regained our breaths, he slid free and eased off the bed. "I'll get a washcloth."

"It's okay." I pushed myself up to shaking feet. I shuffled past Austin, needing a minute alone to process everything that had just happened, so I shut myself in the bathroom and braved the mirror.

My hair had fallen out of its tie and was hanging loose and damp over my shoulders. My lips were red and puffy. And there was something in my eyes, something I hadn't noticed before today.

Love.

I was in love with Austin.

How would I ever pretend like this hadn't happened?

That was tomorrow's worry. I wasn't letting it wreck what we had today, so I cleaned myself up and returned to the bedroom.

Austin was beneath the covers, one strong arm behind his head. The other open and waiting.

I didn't speak as I slipped beneath the covers and curled into his side. His free arm wrapped around my shoulders and pulled me closer. Then I closed my eyes and let the rhythm of his heartbeat seep into my soul. "Merry Christmas."

He kissed my hair and pulled me tighter into his embrace. "Merry Christmas."

CHAPTER NINE

AUSTIN

"Where are you going?" I tightened my hold on Cleo before she could escape the bed.

"I didn't think you were awake."

My eyes were closed, but I'd been awake for hours, savoring the feel of her in my arms and the caress of her hair as it draped across my skin. "I'm not."

"Go back to sleep." Her giggle tickled my chest. "I'm going to find us some lunch."

"Don't go." I wrapped both arms around her, holding her close. "Not yet."

"We'll have to leave this bed at some point."

She was right. Eventually we'd have to face reality. But at the moment, I didn't give a damn about anything except her naked breasts against my ribs and her legs tangled with mine. "Let's just order room service. In ten minutes."

"Okay." She nodded and snuggled deeper.

Being with Cleo . . . there weren't words to describe how well two people fit together. Never in my life had there been a woman like her and never would there be another. She'd destroyed me. She'd changed the path of my life. I wasn't sure what we were going to do but giving her up wasn't an option.

"What are we going to do?" she asked, plucking the thought from my head.

"We'll figure it out. Just know this. Now that I've had you in my arms, I'm not letting you go."

Cleo shifted and propped up on an elbow. "Austin, what's happening here?"

I lifted a hand to tuck a lock of her hair away from her eye. "Damn, you are beautiful."

Her cheeks flushed and her eyes sparkled in the light streaming through the window. Her skin was so smooth and creamy. I bent to kiss the freckle on her collarbone.

She tapped me on the shoulder. "Are you going to answer my question?"

I chuckled, leaning back. There was a crease between her eyebrows, her face etched in worry. "Do you think there are any of your muffins from yesterday in the kitchen? I'd kill for one right now. Or a scone. Or anything that you made yesterday."

She blinked, worry morphing to confusion. "But you hate my food."

"I love your food."

"No, you don't." She frowned. "Don't pretend to like it just because you've seen me naked."

I laughed again, thinking of all the times I'd swallowed a chuckle when she was around. Cleo was one of the funniest, wittiest people in the world, but like her food, I hadn't let myself enjoy her humor.

Shifting, I sat up and leaned against the headboard, my legs stretched down the length of the bed as she sat up to look at me, bringing the sheet with her.

"My favorite is your chocolate cupcakes," I said. "The plain ones, not the ones with the peanut butter filling. Though those are amazing too, the simple chocolate is my favorite. You gave Blake a box for his birthday and I've never been more jealous."

"Is this a joke?"

"No. I want them for my birthday this year."

"Really?"

"Really." I nodded. "They're the best thing I've had in my mouth. Except you, baby."

A smile tugged at the corner of her mouth. "Okay."

"My next favorite are your muffins. Any kind. Though the morning muffin with the carrots and raisins might be tied for top spot with the blueberry."

Her eyes softened. "I've never seen you eat the morning muffin."

"I have."

"When?"

I shrugged. "Whenever you sent stuff with the guys on

duty. But I don't let myself eat much of anything you bake."

"Why?"

"Because it would give too much away. I worried that if I showed how much I loved your food, everyone would see."

"See what?"

"That I'm in love with you."

Her breath hitched. "Austin."

"I love you, Cleo." Saying the words loosened something in my chest. Something that I'd been holding in for far too long. "I've been in love with you since the day I walked into the bakery and spotted you, covered in flour and blueberry stains on your fingers."

"But that was . . ." Her forehead furrowed. The beginning. I'd been in love with her from the beginning. "All this time?"

I nodded, bringing a hand to cup her cheek. There was no use pretending. We were in this together now, vulnerabilities and all. "I need this job with your father. My team, my family, they depend on me. It was easier in a lot of ways to just stay away from you. Pretend it would go away. But it never did. And now there's no pretending. I'm not giving you up."

"I'm not giving you up either." Cleo brushed her fingers through my hair, letting them drop and curve around the shell of my ear.

Her touch was electric. My cock stirred beneath the

sheet and I stretched for her, but she spun off the bed before I could pin her to the mattress, taking the sheet and leaving me stark naked. The quilt was somewhere on the floor.

She swiped her phone from the nightstand and started punching at the screen. Then it flew to her ear as she spun around, realizing that I was naked.

Working out was a regular part of my life and I worked hard to keep my body in shape, mostly for the job but also because exercise helped me sort shit in my head. Cleo's appreciation was a nice bonus.

Her eyes widened as they drifted down my flat stomach to my growing arousal.

I smirked.

"Hi, Dad."

My smirk dropped and I leapt off the bed, rounding the end and grabbing her towel from where we'd dropped it earlier. Then I wrapped it around my waist because there was no way I could be naked in the same room as Cleo while she was talking to Ray.

He said something on the other end of the line that made her roll her eyes.

"I understand you're upset. Get over it."

I blinked, surprised by the sharpness in her tone. I'd never heard Cleo speak to Ray with that kind of defiance.

Good for her.

"I'll be back tomorrow. But there's something important I need to speak to you about and it can't wait."

"Cleo—" I started, but she shot me a look and held up a finger, so I shut up.

Ray was lecturing on the other end of the line. Whatever he was saying, Cleo wasn't listening.

"*Dad*," she barked. "Shush."

Ray's voice grew louder, his frustration coming through loud and clear.

Cleo ripped the phone away from her ear and ended the call. "Grr. I just wanted—"

The phone rang in her hand and she answered it immediately. No doubt it was Ray. "I'm going to hang up on you again unless you can promise to be quiet and listen to me until I'm done."

There was a long pause, then Cleo's shoulders relaxed. "Thank you. Like I was saying, I have something important to tell you."

My stomach knotted.

I was about to get fired.

No matter what Cleo said to Ray, it was inevitable. I'd lose my job and we'd scramble at Garrison. I'd cut my salary and take on any job I could get to make sure the guys had work, even if that meant adding celebrities to my client list. I hated their drama and the goddamn paparazzi, but I wasn't about to sink my company. Channing might have to take some loans out for school but it wasn't the end of the world.

I held my breath, waiting.

Cleo turned to me, the phone pressed to her ear, and smiled. "I'm in love with Austin."

Her words hit me square in the heart. No matter what happened, hearing those words was worth it. Job be damned. She was all I really needed.

I reached out a hand and took hers.

She laced her fingers through mine and her smile stretched wider. "I love him, Dad. And I have for a long time. I'm going to be with Austin."

For the rest of her life, if I had anything to say about it. We weren't there yet. This was hours old, though years in the making. But soon. I'd waited long enough. It was time to throw myself into her life, full force.

"I know this is unexpected, but please—" She pulled the phone away from her ear and gritted her teeth. "He hung up on me."

My phone on my nightstand buzzed.

"It's him." She sighed.

"Yeah." I dropped her hand and went to the other side of the bed and answered Ray's call.

"How long have you been screwing my daughter?"

"That's not any of your business."

"It sure as hell is my business. I pay you to protect her, not to—"

"I quit."

Cleo gasped and slapped a hand to her mouth.

"Goodbye, Ray." I ended the call and tossed my phone aside.

Fuck. That had deteriorated quickly.

"Oh my God, I shouldn't have called him." Cleo's hands dove into her hair as she paced beside the bed. "I'm so sorry. Austin, I'm so sorry. We could have kept it a secret and he wouldn't have known."

"I'm not keeping this a secret."

"But—"

"No more secrets, baby."

Her hands fell and she faced me. "Okay."

"We'll be fine."

The phone rang in her hand and she looked at the screen. She hesitated, taking a long moment before accepting the call. "Yes?"

Ray's voice echoed as he launched into another lecture. I didn't catch it all but he was basically calling into question her life choices.

She closed her eyes, her frame tensing with every passing second. The fingers on her free hand curled into a fist. "Stop! Just stop. When did you become this person? When did you stop hearing me? I know you love me and want what's best for me, but this is my decision. I love Austin. This wasn't something we've been hiding from you for years. We haven't been sneaking around your back. This trip to Montana brought us together and I'm not going to apologize. I love him. And if you accept his resignation, you might as well accept mine too. I quit as your daughter."

I fought a grin. Cleo loved Ray, despite their differences. She might have quit Christmas, but she'd never quit as his daughter. The threat was made, but we all knew it wasn't going to last.

Just like I knew Ray was about to cave.

He loved Cleo more than life.

His reply was muffled, but when her fingers uncurled and her shoulders dropped from her ears, I knew he'd heard her.

"Yes, we can discuss it later," she said. "But not tomorrow. We're coming home and then I'm going to the bakery to make Austin some cupcakes. We'll come for dinner the night after that."

Fuck, but I loved her.

"Okay. Bye, Dad. Merry Christmas." She ended the call, set the phone aside and shrugged. "Neither of us are allowed to quit."

I threw my head back and laughed, then rounded the bed and took her into my arms. "I love you."

"I love you too." Cleo wrapped her arms around my waist, pressing her ear to my heart. "Want me to order room service?"

"Not yet." I gripped the sheet draped around her body and tugged it away before doing the same for my towel. "Merry Christmas, Cleo."

She stood on her toes, smiling against my lips as she ran her hand up my thigh. "Merry Christmas, Austin."

It was one we'd never forget.

———

"I THINK we should come back here," Cleo said, glancing around the lobby of The Eloise Inn. The smile on her face had been there all morning. As we'd showered together. As we'd packed. As we'd checked out of room 410. And now as we waited for the hotel's shuttle to drive us to the airport.

"I like Quincy." She leaned her head against my shoulder. "Maybe we could make it an annual thing. We could come here every Christmas."

"Every third."

"Every other," she countered.

I'd come here every winter and freeze my ass off if that was what she wanted. "Every fourth."

"That's not how compromise works."

I chuckled. "I'll give you every third Christmas with summer trips in between."

She held out her hand. "Agreed."

I took her hand and brought her knuckles to my lips just as the shuttle pulled up. We'd come back to Quincy, of that I had no doubt.

I owed this town, this hotel, my future.

I owed Quincy for Cleo.

EPILOGUE
CLEO

Two years later...

"That is not what we agreed on, Austin."

"Yes, it is." He had his hands on his hips as he stood across from me in the bakery's kitchen.

"No, it isn't." I bounced our son on my hip and took a calming breath. "You said chocolate."

"I said vanilla."

"No, you didn't."

"I did, baby. I said vanilla."

He took one of my chocolate cupcakes from the box and swiped his finger through the frosting. A slow grin spread across his face as he licked it off. "But I'll take these to the office. The guys will eat them."

"You lying—" I stretched for the rag on the counter, ready to throw it at his face, but Austin was faster. He snatched it away before I could nab it.

Shaun cooed before shoving his fist into his mouth, coating his knuckles with drool.

I marched to the fridge and flung the door open, taking out one of his teething rings. He wasn't teething yet, but he loved to put things in his mouth and I preferred the sanitized toys to his chubby fingers. I handed it to him and dried off his fist.

While I took care of our son, Austin inhaled a cupcake, one I'd made specifically for his mother.

She was working on Christmas Day and Austin had wanted to bring her something sweet tonight. Sweet was where I shined so I'd promised to take care of it with a half dozen chocolate cupcakes, minus sprinkles or filling. That's what he'd asked for, something I recalled with clarity because those were his favorite cupcakes. I should have known he'd been up to something to score extra cupcakes. We'd been so busy preparing for the holidays, I hadn't brought any of his favorites home for the past two weeks.

The door to the kitchen opened and Brynne breezed in. "Phew. I just flipped the sign and locked the door."

"Thank you." I gave her a smile. "Today was crazy."

The Christmas Eve rush we'd expected had kept us busy all day. We'd nearly run out of everything in the display case, though luckily, there were plenty of vanilla cupcakes out there for me to steal for Austin's mom. My husband would hoard the chocolate for himself because there was no way he'd share those with his team. The man would run an extra two miles every day this week just to eat all six cupcakes.

"Would you mind putting together a box of six vanilla before you go home?" I asked Brynne.

"Not at all." She came closer and tickled Shaun's foot.

I could get the cupcakes myself, but I didn't want to let Shaun go yet. He'd been home with Austin all day while I'd been at work and I'd missed him.

At three months old, Shaun was already a miniature version of Austin. They had the same dark hair and coffee-brown eyes. Shaun's nose looked more like mine, but he was little and who knew how he'd change as he grew.

"How was he today?" I asked Austin.

"Good." He licked the last bit of frosting from his thumb, then threw the cupcake wrapper in the trash. "We didn't do much. He played in his Jumperoo while I did a workout. Then we took a nap. He's kind of been fussy today and his nose is runny. Maybe he's getting a cold."

"Poor baby." I kissed the top of his head. "Let's use it as an excuse to duck out of the party early."

"Fine by me."

We were going to my father's house tonight for his annual Christmas Eve celebration. The last thing I wanted to do was get dressed up after being at the bakery since four, but Dad had begged for us to come.

Austin's mom was coming to our house to spend the evening babysitting Shaun, then tomorrow, we were having a quiet Christmas morning at our house before everyone came over for dinner to celebrate the baby's first Christmas.

The only thing I was looking forward to tonight was seeing Austin in a suit. The man was gorgeous in whatever he wore, but in his black suit, I'd struggle to keep my hands off him until we were home.

It had been the same on our wedding day. We'd had a quickie on the drive from the church to the reception in the back of our limo, hidden by the privacy screen from the driver, because I hadn't been able to resist.

We'd gotten married last year, a week before Christmas. The ceremony had been simple and elegant. My stepmother had, of course, wanted an extravagant party, but we'd kept the ceremony and reception small. Then we'd escaped all the holiday madness because Austin had whisked me away to Quincy for our honeymoon. We'd asked to stay in the same room and had ordered room service for five days straight, rarely leaving the bed.

He'd knocked me up in that room.

I rounded the table and came to Austin's side.

He put his arm around my shoulders and pulled me into a hug. "Tired?"

I nodded and hummed, leaning into his broad chest. "Yeah. I really don't want to go to this party tonight. Next year, let's go somewhere."

"Actually . . ." He reached into the diaper bag on the

table, fishing around the front pocket until he came out with a piece of paper.

A receipt.

For a room at The Eloise Inn.

"What is this?"

"Your Christmas Eve gift. We're leaving the day after Christmas for Quincy."

"Really?"

He nodded. "Your dad offered up the plane. My mom has to work anyway so we agreed to celebrate when we get home. Channing is spending the week at his girlfriend's place. So we're escaping."

It sounded perfect.

We'd been so busy lately, with work and life, a break, just the three of us, was long overdue.

Austin had quit working for my father after all. It had become a conflict of interest and he'd decided it was best to keep his business separate from my family. Of course, Dad completely disagreed, but given the fact that I was living with my own personal bodyguard, he'd eventually realized it was the right move.

Replacing Dad's income hadn't been any trouble for Austin after all. Thanks to a couple of glowing referrals from my father, Garrison had taken on several large clients and was poised to have its biggest year yet. In the past two years, Austin's team had doubled and he'd scrambled to expand to meet his growing client list. He'd put in a lot of long hours over the past twenty-four months, but we were finally settling into a routine. We were finally in a good place to take this vacation.

Brynne poked her head inside the door. "Did you tell her?"

"Yep." Austin grinned.

"Good." She walked in with the box of vanilla cupcakes. "I almost blurted it out today. Twice. I suck at keeping secrets."

"You knew?"

She nodded. "You need a vacation. I've got this place covered."

"Thank you." I tipped my head up to Austin. "And thank you."

He dropped his lips to mine. "Love you."

"I love you too."

Shaun threw his teething ring on the floor and took a chunk of my hair in his fist.

"What do you think, buddy?" Austin unwound his fingers. "Ready to go to Montana?"

Our son let out a loud coo before opening his mouth as wide as possible and inserting his fist.

Austin kissed his hair, then did the same to mine before letting us go. We loaded up the diaper bag and locked the bakery doors.

Then we went home to pack for another Christmas in Quincy.

———

Want more of Quincy and the Eden family? The Eden series continues with Indigo Ridge.

ACKNOWLEDGMENTS

Thank you for reading *Christmas in Quincy*! Stay tuned for more stories set in this charming town. Special thanks to my editing and proofreading team: Elizabeth Nover, Julie Deaton, and Judy Zweifel. And thank you to Sarah Hansen for the beautiful cover.

Merry Christmas & Happy Holidays!

ABOUT THE AUTHOR

Devney is a *USA Today* bestselling author who lives in Washington with her husband and two sons. Born and raised in Montana, she loves writing books set in her treasured home state. After working in the technology industry for nearly a decade, she abandoned conference calls and project schedules to enjoy a slower pace at home with her family. Writing one book, let alone many, was not something she ever expected to do. But now that she's discovered her true passion for writing romance, she has no plans to ever stop.

Don't miss out on Devney's latest book news.
Subscribe to her newsletter!
www.devneyperry.com